CITY HALL

CASTLE ROCK ENTERTAINMENT PRESENTS AN EDWARD R. PRESSMAN/KEN LIPPER PRODUCTION A HAROLD BECKER FILM

AL PACINO JOHN CUSACK BRIDGET FONDA DANNY AIELLO "CITY HALL" DAVID PAYMER AND MARTIN LANDAU MUSIC BY JERRY GOLDSMITH

EDITED BY ROBERT C. JONES AND DAVID BRETHERTON PRODUCTION DESIGNER JANE MUSKY DIRECTOR OF PHOTOGRAPHY MICHAEL SERESIN WRITTEN BY KEN LIPPER PAUL SCHRADER NICHOLAS PILEGGI AND BO GOLDMAN

PRODUCED BY EDWARD R. PRESSMAN, KEN LIPPER, CHARLES MULVEHILL AND HAROLD BECKER DIRECTED BY HAROLD BECKER

COLUMBIA PICTURES

DOLBY

CASTLE ROCK

CITY HALL

KEN LIPPER

Based on the Motion Picture Written by Ken Lipper and
Paul Schrader & Nicholas Pileggi and Bo Goldman

St. Martin's Paperbacks

CITY HALL

ISBN: 0-312-95906-0

Printed in the United States of America

St. Martin's Paperbacks edition/February 1996

10 9 8 7 6 5 4 3 2 1

City Hall is dedicated to my late beloved brother and mother, Jerry and Sally, without whom the best achievements in my life would not have been possible.

CHAPTER ONE

New York. The sweater of government was unraveling. And the cities of New York seemed ready to explode. It all began routinely enough with a shooting: one of 2,000 murders a year; 165 a month; six a day. This was just one of them.

Every sunrise was a victory for Edgar Bone. The only dream he had left was for his son to survive each day and night, until they could afford to escape Bushwick. Bone ached with anger knowing that the silent indifference of the white community allowed neither law nor order to exist in the ghetto, so long as the murderous violence stayed within borders sharply defined by race and poverty. The affront was all the more personal, when Bone recalled the Silver Star he received in Vietnam, by almost dying for the complacent folks who ignored him now.

Bone's disillusionment was more hurtful than bitter. His experience with white folks in the workplace, as Marine Staff Sergeant and now as a Kings County Hospital lab technician, ran contrary to the collective daily pain and danger he felt as any black man in the streets of New York. Deep within his soul, Bone loved all people. And to avoid the despair wrought by spiritual isolation, he needed desperately to believe in them.

That rainy Monday morning, after fastening Robby's slicker, Bone carefully opened his apartment door to escort his son to school. Ghetto chimes—successive locks clicking open, chains sliding free, and a heavy bar being lifted—resounded in the dimly lit hallway. Cockroaches the size of quarters crawled the walls with an imperial air that came from their immunity. The Bones zigged and zagged down the long, narrow corridors of Carver Houses, appearing from a distance as cartoonlike football players moving in a broken field pattern. The zigging and zagging was part of a deadly game to avoid stepping on the crack vials, syringes, and used condoms that carpeted the floor.

A *modus vivendi* existed in the city's housing projects. At night crack addicts, junkies, whores, and perverts owned the hallways and staircases, while decent families were in the habit of becoming prisoners behind barricaded doors. By morning the occupiers slithered back to their netherworld, leaving wretched artifacts.

Robby playfully wove a sharp U-turn and tripped over a sleeping body too strung out to retreat. It coiled toward the boy. Burnt-out red eyes caught a glimpse of Bone's enormous hands and muscular body tensed over him, just before a karate kick slammed him into the stone floor. The addict pissed in his pants, adding fresh urine to the insistent, putrid stench that penetrated every pore of Carver Houses' public spaces.

None of the neatly dressed "day people" who hurried to work over the paths that dissected the project were exceptional. They plodded through life taking orders as part of the stolid service peasantry that made New York's hospitals, cafeterias, government agencies and financial back offices grind along. Time and abortive efforts proved that life just happened to them, so they didn't spend much energy trying to influence it. Each day was like reliving the day before. Too many joyless faces starting the day with the hope that it would be over quickly; some already deadening the monotony with predawn vodka.

The social contact Carver residents had with the white community was far less than that of a single United Nations ambassador. It was one thing to be poor and loved and another to be poor and unloved. These were children of a city that did not love them . . . and they felt it.

Eyes swept the floor. Carver dwellers stopped to talk to no one, because death came suddenly to project people; shootouts mushroomed from a foul on the basketball court, unpaid debts, bad drugs peddled the night before, or just an accidental bumping of bodies. The operating principle was to shoot before someone shoots you.

Bone's conversation with his six-year-old son turned to gentle admonition:

"Dad, can't I go to the playground after school?"

"No . . . sorry, the playground is no place for a little boy."

A few miles away, Detective Santos' electric energy contrasted with his decaying surroundings in the 101st precinct, as well as with the weariness weighing on the returning midnight-to-eight patrol. Ignoring his own fatigue, which came as much from the futility of his mission as its physical effort, Santos raced by a too-tall desk, once supposed to intimidate those forced to look up at the bored sergeant manning it. The officer muttered, "Don't you ever go home, Santos?" more in annoyance than admiration.

"Gotta meet a snitch at the Carver Houses," Eddie replied without breaking stride.

"Cops like you are the first to die, you know," he said grinning. "It's a naked fact."

"You gotta live until you die, Sarge. Cops either eat shit or dish it out."

Eddie Santos was the toughest cop in Brooklyn North, which policed Bushwick, East New York, Williamsburg, and Red Hook, the city's meanest streets. These neighborhoods were so drowned in shootings that one would have imagined there was a revolution, if the homicides were not so clearly pointless.

Santos was cunning, a stickler for detail, fanatical and violent. As a child of New York's untamed streets he feared no one. The bigger the criminal, the more he fixated on running him down.

Eddie's reputation was not built on the number of arrests he made, rather the likelihood of their resulting in convictions. In a city which had 428,000 *reported* felonies a year, 140,000 arrests leading to only 45,940 indictments, 39,000 plea bargains and a stunningly skinny 2,120 trial convictions, it was remarkable that Detective Santos' penchant for patient stalking resulted in cases with thirty times that conviction rate.

The streetlamp silhouette of Eddie Santos' broad shoulders tapering to his narrow waist, piled on thick legs seemingly anchored to the ground under them, struck terror into the most vicious predator. Word on the street was that when Santos lay in ambush for you, you either died or did hard jail time.

Santos hated the drug dealers and the revolving-door justice system that allowed them to destroy young lives. Their ugly residue continually intruded on his sensibilities. The 101 played host to scores of low-level drug dealers, addicts, prostitutes, and gun runners, a long line chained together at the wrists each night, herded into grim holding pens layered with puke, piss, and human excrement. A couple of the regulars pointed curse fingers toward a steel door with a tinted glass window, at which youthful undercover narcs identified the perps who sold to them during buy-and-bust operations.

Light-skinned blond teenagers always stood out among the predominantly African-American population that inhabited Brooklyn North cells. As the father of a daughter and a son, Santos was particularly disturbed by these teenage drug addicts, who had only weeks ago stepped off a bus clean, from wherever it was in middle America that they ran away from. Such children were regularly approached at the Port Authority bus station by voracious pimps promising care and friendship to these frightened, lonely children, only to hook them on drugs and a brief life of prostitution.

Santos instinctively knew that Calcutta in New York couldn't exist with immunity right up to the kingpin suppliers and money men, unless high-level political and judicial corruption extended a veil of protection over their criminal enterprises. And this morning, Detective Eddie Santos had a chance to do something about it.

He drove his unmarked black Ford police special through the seemingly eternal rain. The vehicle turned from Broadway onto Marcy Street and skidded to a stop in front of an all-night pool hall, from which a slight, unshaven, long-haired punk emerged and jumped into Santos' car.

Despite Vinnie Zapatti's swagger, high boots, heavy metal buckles, and strap-laden leather jacket, he still looked more like the errand boy for wiseguys that he was, than a tough hood. Vinnie's "respect" came from his being the nephew of mob boss Paul Zapatti. That is also why he was of interest to Eddie, who had recently nailed Vinnie cold on this third felony drug charge, one that could send him up for life . . . unless, of course, he delivered a bigger fish into Detective Santos' net. That fish was his cousin Tino Zapatti, who amazingly had been released on probation by a judge after Detective Santos had busted him for selling cocaine and possessing a loaded gun in front of an elementary school.

"Where we gonna meet Tino?" Santos asked icily.

"A few blocks from here, by the broken bench in front of the Carver housing project," Vinnie practically whispered, cowering against the car door.

"What are you doing way over there, Vinnie?" Santos asked tauntingly.

"I can't stand cops." Vinnie spoke without heart, in a vain attempt to affirm a non-existent manhood to himself.

"But if you hate cops, why do you do bad things? Bad things interest cops."

"A few bullshit ounces and—" Santos cut him off.

"And three strikes you're out. That's the law now. Three felony convictions means life. It's numbers. These days you can't beat the numbers, Vinnie."

". . . They'll find me. My uncle will find me."

"Witness protection, they don't find anybody. It helps us . . . and it helps scum like you and Tino."

Vinnie twisted like hooked bait facing certain death. "You're not taking him in?! You said you weren't taking him in. I'm dead."

Vinnie grasped the door handle in a gesture to escape, as Santos clamped his large hand viselike over Vinnie's and jerked him back by his collar with the other one.

"Easy. I just want to have a little chat with Tino. I hear he's carrying a gun again. That's breaking probation. But I don't want to take him in. Just pressure him to talk to me . . . about certain things he knows. Like you."

"Now don't fuck me. Tino's on his way. He don't know nothing what it's about. You're going to bump into us by accident," Vinnie whimpered. "Right?"

"Here comes our boy," Santos noted with tense anticipation. A tall, hulking figure walked quickly down Broadway and turned the corner, his nervous eyes darting in every direction. A silver bombardier jacket was zipped only about four inches from its hem and Tino's black shirt stuck soaking wet to his hard body. Tino's bottomless eyes and expressionless face created a lifeless effect.

"Now don't get excited, Vinnie, we're just going to talk to him."

Vinnie sat frozen as Santos placed a powerful hand around his throat and pressed.

"Life in prison . . . or get the fuck out of the

car . . . And turn him around, so his back faces me."

Santos shoved him into the driving rain; Vinnie was trembling so hard that Santos could practically still hear him shaking.

Bone and Robby emerged from their building doorway and the father protectively wrapped the child's hand in his own, as they walked together along a project path toward Broadway.

Tino sensed somebody approaching him from behind and turned to spot Vinnie.

"Hey, Vinnie," he shouted in accepting familiarity, and stuck up his right hand to slap him a high five. Everything about Tino wreaked of death. As Vinnie turned and touched Tino, he felt only death—his death—and he panicked big time. Lunging past Tino, Vinnie broke into a hysterical sprint toward Eddie, unexpectedly exposing Detective Santos face-to-face with a turned-on killing machine. Their eyes met in a terrible, hate-filled moment of recognition; Santos instinctively knew that Tino had the drop on him and would erase his life. Tino's body burned with the fires of death as he mechanically reached into his belt, drew a 9 millimeter pistol, and, feeling nothing, fired three bullets point-blank into Detective Eddie Santos' exposed chest.

Santos' body was stunned by the bullets

tearing through his flesh; Eddie's heart spouted blood like a split water main as life drained out of him. Then as Eddie slumped in slow motion to the rain- and blood-soaked pavement, a demonic force shaped Santos' blood-stained hand around the revolver in his ankle holster, which he fluidly drew and fired twice. A single bullet ripped open Tino's throat, drilling a gaping see-through hole. Tino, an insane "top of the world, Ma" grin pasted to his blood-spattered face, spun like a top with his finger locked on the automatic's trigger, firing wildly in every direction.

Carver Houses was Sarajevo, with briefcases, groceries, and newspapers sprayed onto its dirt yard; grass reseeding had long been dispensed with by city budget cuts. Dozens of men and women flattened as close to earth as physics would permit. Bone and Robby walked into the midst of this macabre street theatre. And the father's whole being instantaneously incorporated the explosions, in time to subconsciously comprehend his son's tiny palm melting from his grip.

Father covered limp child with his own body until silence engulfed the moment. He rose to his knees and cradled the boy, first breathing and then praying life back into him. He stared in helpless despair, knowing that the bullet in Robby's forehead had snatched everything from him. Bone moaned repetitiously from an ancient well, punching the cracked asphalt pavement with his massive, bleeding fists, heavy tears rolling down his smooth, brown face.

Blue-and-whites flew up Broadway, down obscure cross streets, going the wrong way on one-ways, with sirens cutting Brooklyn apart. Squad cars swarmed over the project's grounds, which were already cratered by neglect. Radios crackled their alarm incessantly:

"All units: Ten-thirteen, Carver Houses. Assist patrolman. MOF down, member of the force down. . . !"

Police Commissioner Coonan remembered every incident of a cop gunned down on his watch. And he fumed at the thought of his men murdered, because they probably hesitated a second too long with some crack-crazed killers. Coonan hated those civic-minded grand juries that indicted his cops for brutality, even murder, from the hindsight which flourished in their orderly courthouse sanctuaries.

"MOF down . . . member of the force down. . . ," kept intruding into the lurching squad cars. After thirty-four years with New York's finest, Coonan thought he was ready to retire. All of his best cops would soon be working in Suffolk or Greenwich anyway. Those who stayed on the force would turn their backs on crime, knowing they would be outgunned or second-guessed.

Before leaving his patrol car, the commissioner made a conscious effort to regain his composure. The spin, control boys at headquarter's public relations had tutored the brass that television was a cool medium on which anger played poorly, even with a dying cop.

A burly, red-faced inspector pulled Coonan away from the crowd, which had taken on a showbiz air: reporters pleading for details and TV cameramen elbowing still photographers and radio interviewers for position.

Coonan quizzed his inspector on what happened.

"Detective Santos got it . . . probably a drug bust gone bad."

"What about his back-up?"

"He was alone!"

"Alone? What the hell was he doing meeting with drug dealers alone?"

"There's no record of an assignment . . . doesn't mean anything," the inspector said with more hope than conviction.

"I don't like it. Violates procedure. Notify Internal Affairs," he ordered, his heavy voice expressing concern and sadness.

"Yes sir."

"Who was the shooter?"

"Headquarters didn't need to check the computer, once I gave the name . . . Tino Zapatti."

"That Zapatti?"

"Yup, Paul Zapatti's nephew."

"At least Santos didn't ice a boy scout." The commissioner was enough of a politician to know that he was handling political dynamite.

"You stall the press. I'll give the mayor a heads-up."

CHAPTER TWO

A million miles removed from Bone cradling his dead son in Bushwick, Mayor of New York John Pappas, protected by his two regular bodyguards from the elite police Intelligence Unit, made his way carefully down the stone steps in front of a glistening white Victorian City Hall. Today's cold driving December rain had left an invisible slick on the steep steps of government, making them unpredictably hazardous to navigate.

Familiar homeless residents sprawling on the benches of City Hall Park, and civil servants rushing to work in the nearby Municipal Building, hardly noticed eight dozen chanting demonstrators waving banners at the mayor.

But with different groups protesting each day, Mayor Pappas couldn't help thinking that City Hall Park contained the chaos of the universe, before God spent seven days putting it in order. Unlike God, however, Mayor Pappas was a prisoner of limited resources. Tough economic times, federal cuts, and austere budgets meant that he could offer no, or at best only partial, solutions to even legitimate problems.

Today's protest permits had been issued to groups that illustrated the contrast between the high public expectations from government and the low tolerance for communal sacrifice; workers against layoffs at municipal hospitals; parents demanding modern, safe schools; and construction workers objecting to higher real estate taxes that might threaten their jobs and the interests of pudgy landlords sitting dry in their Park Avenue offices. When the protestors booed him, Mayor Pappas mechanically smiled and waved to them, knowing that a concerned fatherly appearance was often as important as a solution in elective politics, while grumbling to the Intel man beside him, "Unfortunately, it takes $165 in airfare to yell at a senator in Washington and only a subway token to hassle the mayor."

Mayor Pappas proceeded around the back of City Hall, where he was to meet with Frank

Anselmo, boss of New York City's Democratic party. Every since Congressman Biaggi and Party Boss Esposito were convicted by the Feds through electronic eavesdropping, Anselmo insisted on conducting all serious business face-to-face outdoors. In his line of business, where the reality of power depended as much on appearance as on tangible deeds, reports of "hiding" important things or "secret negotiations" in the park only added to Anselmo's mystique and aura of influence.

As the mayor turned the corner of City Hall, he could see Anselmo restlessly pacing and splashing along the park path, in the shadow of the Tweed Courthouse. In perspective, everything about this tall man in his sixties looked roundish. A fleshy head rested on slightly slouching shoulders, which led into long arms forming an arc with Anselmo's modest soft paunch. Anselmo described his political philosophy the way he looked: "Political decisions are points on an ellipse; there are no right angles." He always seemed ready to embrace you, but his lively, alert eyes signaled there was a price to be paid for his affection.

Anselmo and Pappas were close personal friends, mostly political allies, although sometimes governmental foes. Boss and mayor accepted the fact that friendship could become too heavy a burden when carried into professional decision making, where public interest, self-interest, and organization survival are necessarily the guideposts. And within these parameters, each man had his own order of priorities and limits.

The mayor still had fresh eyes for democracy and felt a need to get into people's heads and hearts. And he admired people with convictions. While none of those things impeded his practical bent for the horse trading required to get immediate things done, John Pappas always hung these idealistic views in front of him.

Anselmo, on the other hand, was convinced that there was too much democracy; crowds with too many convictions and too few solutions. Believers were self-righteous, often impossible to deal with, thereby limiting the little practical progress which politicians could make. Deals were the oxygen big cities breathed on; those who understood loyalty or had self-interest at stake made for stable and predictable partners and opposition.

. Anselmo's jovial demeanor had been replaced with a scowl.

"Mr. Big Shot. Now that you're mayor it's okay to keep me waiting in the rain," Anselmo said, immediately putting his adversary on the defensive.

"Sorry. Important call from Washington about—"

Anselmo interrupted him.

"Fuck Washington! It's those mothers marching in the rain to get their kids decent schools"—piercing the wet air with his index finger in the direction of the protestors—"who get you elected. Why did you kill the school construction bill?"

Deputy Mayor Calhoun, a numbers man to the core, had convinced Pappas that New York's credit could not bear the heavy borrowing necessary to fund the school construction legislation which Anselmo had introduced in the City Council, without losing its bond ratings with Standard & Poor's and Moody's. Now John Pappas had hardly heard of these agencies, which effectively decided how much the City could borrow, and at what interest rate, toward funding the four billion dollars of municipal bonds it was requried to issue annually to pay for public works. But as every mayor before him had learned, wherever you start ideologically, left or right, the stability demanded by these nongovernmental credit watchdogs forced you to the center.

"I love schools as much as anyone. But I don't have the money for so many new ones. And Calhoun says that each school is over-engineered, with expensive bells and whistles."

Anselmo shot back, "You against kids getting the best education?"

"Let's get real, Frank. This isn't about kids or education . . . we're arguing about contracts, and contractors who contribute to your party organization."

The mayor's cynical tone deepened as he continued.

"The construction program specifies boilers that could run a nuclear plant; air conditioning for elementary schools that are closed during the summer; and triple-paned soundproof windows for buildings located on quiet side streets. What do they all have in common? Nothing that advances the safety, comfort, or education of kids. No! Just high profit margins for the contractors."

Disgust permeated Anselmo's reply:

"Contractors who gave the campaign contributions which got you elected. Remember? Where's your loyalty? You and our other candidates are going to need them to get reelected next year, for God's sakes." Then his tone became grave. "And there's tremendous pressure from the school boards and PTAs."

"We're broke. You have to put this off," responded Mayor Pappas, quiet eyes falling toward the ground as an indication that he took no pleasure from his opposition role.

Loyalty! Anselmo had a fanatic belief that loyalty to the party organization was the foundation of order in this urban cauldron. Absent a permanent government, politics would fall into the unruly hands of transient demagogues who, lacking a permanent constituency, would obstruct government, without any obligation to produce. Anselmo didn't favor one constituency; his role was to dispense benefits in a balanced fashion, so that every constituency got enough to have a stake in the existing order.

Anselmo loved to reminisce about his days as a petitioner for Carmine DeSapio, proudly reciting his political dictum of "everything for my friends, the law for my enemies." It was enough for them to say, "Vote for my man, he's a Democrat," because voters understood the implicit covenant. Democrats would of course take care of their own, but they could also be counted on to provide jobs and schools for working families. Anselmo spoke contemptuously about unfocused mob politics by parroting Yul Brynner's lament in *The King and I*: "Et cetera, et cetera, and so forth." He continued, "Everybody marching to his own drummer, a different drummer: free choice versus right to life, multi-cultural education versus the melting pot, anti-development versus economic growth, save the whales . . ." At this point, he ruefully acknowledged that the Mayor of New York received more mail about animal rights than about protecting children.

While Anselmo and the mayor slugged it out over the school construction standoff, Deptuy Mayor Kevin Calhoun sat in his tiny office plowing through the mountain of paper which government recreated every day. The office looked much as it had during the past 150 years, with a white eighteen-foot ceiling resting on dark crimson walls offset by white trim. Calhoun's antique desk and small oval conference table were buried in official-looking documents, and papers stamped "CONFIDENTIAL" were piled high along every wall, as well as two deep into a now-defunct majestic marble fireplace. The only physically contrasting element in this traditional office were four television sets stacked on a table, so that the deputy mayor could watch the three network and CNN news programs simultaneously.

There were larger offices available at City Hall, but this one shared a common doorway and private hallway to the toilet with the mayor's office. When Mayor Pappas came in or out of the private side to his office, the only person he saw was Calhoun. The mayor asked the same question each time, with a thinly contained fear of anticipation to his voice:

"Anything new, Kevin?"

The deputy mayor knew that physical proximity to the source of power was real power itself. Government power was about access and every politician knew that Calhoun had the first and last word with the mayor each day.

Calhoun had thirty-five lines on his phone, each perpetually lit by incoming calls. Four crack assistants and two secretaries expertly and politely attended to all but the most important callers. Nevertheless, Calhoun remained edgy that something vital was being missed, in this elaborate ballet of telephone triage.

Buzz! Buzz! Buzz! The insistent intercom burrowed into his consciousness. Calhoun quickly broke his train of thought and grasped the receiver. Peggy was the deputy mayor's secretary throughout his eleven years as a researcher and ultimately staff director of the Congressional House Ways and Means Committee, and she could reliably pierce the facade of official authority at any time:

"It's the PC. He says it's urgent and the mayor is out."

"Put him through," Calhoun replied hastily.

The police commissioner maintained his formality.

"Good morning, sir."

"Hope it's good news, Commissioner," Calhoun said with false bravado, now sitting back to see how much the reality would hurt.

"Afraid not, sir. MOF down in the Carver project. Perp's dead."

"Was it racial?" Kevin asked routinely.

"Both the cop and perp were white. But a six-year-old black kid was cut down in the crossfire. Local folks are pretty angry. Ninth black kid killed by random gunfire in Brooklyn this year."

"Shit! Look, I know all your men are excited, with a cop down. Tell them to go easy on the crowd. The last thing we need is a race riot." Kevin's voice was filled with concern.

The police commissioner's tone stiffened as he responded. "We'll keep a lid on things. I'm heading to Kings County Hospital. The press will be swarming all over the place when they learn the rest of the bad news."

"What bad news is that?" the deputy mayor said predictably.

"The shooter was Tino Zapatti, the mafioso's nephew. He was meeting alone with the cop when the incident erupted. The detective was not on an assignment. And there will be a lot of questions," the commissioner said with much certainty and some discouragement.

"The mayor and I will meet you at Kings County. You know it's his policy to be at the bedside of every wounded cop. And thanks for the heads-up, Coonan."

Calhoun slammed the receiver down and raced out of City Hall to find the mayor, who was still engaged in heated discussions with Anselmo over the School Construction Fund. Anselmo was boiling mad at Mayor John Pappas' apparent betrayal of Party organization principles.

"I operate the machine you preside over. I could have elected any Puerto Rican mayor, Juan," emphasizing his pre-anglicized name. "I created you! And now you bite my ass," Anselmo groaned scornfully.

Mayor Pappas' history proved that Anselmo was probably not far from wrong. Juan Pappas was born in Puerto Rico. His father was the first Hispanic building superintendent in Anselmo's all-Italian bastion of Bay Ridge. "Señor Pappas," as Anselmo loved to call him, quickly became a devoted worker for his Democratic Club, insuring 100 percent signed nominating petitions in the buildings he ran. Anselmo personally taught Señor Pappas' six-year-old son, Juan, to petition with a sawed-off broomstick that could reach doorbells, if he stood on his "tippy-tiptoes," as Frank always pressed him to do.

When Juan graduated from Erasmus Hall High School, Anselmo got him a four-year scholarship at Brooklyn Polytechnic University, with a delicately placed alert to the dean of a pending city subsidy for his new science building. During university, Juan's friends casually Americanized his name to John. Upon graduation as a civil engineer, John secured a valued civil service line as a bridge inspector. Since Anselmo had also appointed the transportation commissioner, Pappas' boss gave him flexible time to carry out political tasks for the Democratic party organization.

Pappas climbed the organization ladder to become Commissioner of General Services. Responding to Anselmo's suggestion of tailoring the bid specifications toward a night-construction schedule, Commissioner Pappas helped steer a 150 million dollar competitively bid electrical job on the 59th Street Bridge subway line to a company allegedly controlled by Paul Zapatti, a shadowy figure who reputedly operated carting services, laundries, trucking companies, hotels, and unions, all of whose unquestioned financial and voluntary manpower support around election time strengthened Anselmo's political grip on New

York's party apparatus. Pappas' political skill and loyalty were now undisputed.

As Pappas was scaling the political peaks, Gus Georges, a radical black assemblyman, threatened a mayoral primary against the Democratic organization. Anselmo recognized that the party apparatus could probably defeat Georges this time. But he was shrewd enough to detect that the complexion of New York required some accommodation. He responded with the flexibility of water gently sliding around the rocks that barred its route.

The party boss called a sit-down with minority district leaders, who enjoyed exclusive distribution rights over many of the city's social welfare programs. They trusted Georges' loose-cannon brand of politics even less than Anselmo did. Everyone quickly agreed to nominate a known quantity, an electable minority person with tested links to the organization. John Pappas was perfect.

Anselmo ignored cries to punish Georges for his assault on the organization. Instead, he turned to political bribery in order to make Georges part of the family. The radical smilingly accepted a $25,000 annual lulu, plus anything else that informally came his way in the state legislature, when the party leadership appointed him Chairman of the Public Works Committee.

Although well known among insiders, the public at large had not heard of John Pappas when he was nominated. After a well-financed, well-organized campaign with a reform theme, Pappas was elected New York's first Hispanic mayor. The event was seen differently by various beholders. The press hailed it as a breakthrough for minority representation. Liberals pledged to follow Pappas in carrying out his campaign pledge to inject fairness into New York's sclerotic political decision-making process. Insiders applauded Anselmo's brilliance for anointing Pappas emperor under his regency.

Mayor Pappas had recently turned fifty-five and recognized that this was his last chance to make his life count for something special. He was determined to use his office to serve the people and to make New York again the greatest city in the world.

Anselmo and Pappas continued their negotiations along the paths of City Hall Park. Well aware of his loyalties and the fact that there was considerable public and political need for Anselmo's school construction program, the mayor offered a compromise.

"Frank, we've worked together too long for miscues. I can give you half the schools in this year's budget, half next year. But no frills! There's still enough juice to satisfy your contractors. And we will break ground for a new school in every district you designate, before election day. Go with me Frank. It's the best I can do."

Anselmo quickly recognized that this was indeed the best deal he could get.

"Okay, but what's going on? Everything's become a trade-off."

Deputy Mayor Kevin Calhoun dripped as he ran toward them, without an umbrella. Behind Kevin, the mayor's limousine and a back-up Intel vehicle pulled around City Hall, onto the grass, for a quick departure. Something urgent was demanding the mayor's presence.

Anselmo deliberately raised his voice, so Kevin could hear him.

"The problem is that boy deputy mayor of yours, isn't it? Why should I take crap from him?

Mayor Pappas hugged Anselmo and whispered in his ear, "Because he's my boy. Just like I was your boy."

Anselmo and Pappas smiled warmly, and then the mayor turned to Kevin.

Twelve years earlier, Kevin Calhoun's father, a renowned archeology professor at Columbia University, let go with a cynical laugh when his son said he was joining the Congressional staff:

"Don't waste your time. Man has done, undone, and redone just about everything. Politicans can satisfy their egos and line their pockets, but human nature defies fundamental improvement."

Kevin admired his dad's brilliant dedication to the inert and dead, but he did not wish to inherit his cloistered spirit. He sought a life filled with the warmth and genuine emotion which comes from human encounter; the passion derived from participating in a higher purpose than achieving a spectator's knowledge, even if his lofty goal would remain unfulfilled. The younger Calhoun was certain that mankind could be improved, although he was not sure how to best direct his energies toward implementing that belief. Congress seemed as good a place to start as any.

Kevin was an enormous success in Washington, rising to staff director of the pivotal House Ways and Means Committee. Ironically, his reputation was not built upon passionate engagement with the public, rather as an analytical genius with unique quantitative skills in budget balancing.

Calhoun was growing weary with Washington when he encountered Mayor John Pappas, who was then testifying before Congress to obtain full funding for Head Start. The capital had become obsessed with the limitations of government to help people. More and more congressmen viewed public service as separate from moral purpose, with perpetuation of their power as the goal in itself. In the absence of public purpose, empty rhetoric and vain courtesies increasingly dominated the Congressional hallways.

When the recently elected Mayor of New York addressed the committee, he not only integrated politics with a moral agenda, but the brilliance in his dark eyes peered right through the television camera into people's homes; professionals quickly realized that this short, wavy haired, open-faced Hispanic with a soft, wide smile not only had an agenda, but the leadership skills to get others to follow him.

"We must not be hobbled by our perceived limitations of government. Man is perfectible, and government indeed has both the obligation and means to help perfect him—starting with our children," the mayor had told the committee. Kevin was fascinated to observe that when Mayor Pappas made his points, he forcefully leaned his whole body into the words, like Mickey Mantle swinging for the fences at Yankee Stadium.

Kevin's excitement with government was reignited. He loved Pappas' missionary zeal and the power of his presentation; and he felt that he could fill in the specifics of the agenda better than anyone else. While Washington distributed the money, it was essentially only a pass-through vehicle to the cities and states where funds were spent and programs managed. Kevin Calhoun had already decided that he wanted to join local government, where the rubber hit the road, when he crossed the chamber and introduced himself to Mayor Pappas.

CHAPTER THREE

The mayor hired his new deputy to obtain obvious governmental skills, as well as for his enthusiastic commitment to public service *and* John Pappas. Calhoun stood in stark contrast to the elite New Yorkers, who, with lavish public toasts on election night, promised to join the new mayor in "making war on the status quo," only to uniformly desert his tiny army in formation at the first whiff of combat.

Anselmo and his district leaders objected strongly to bypassing regulars for important commissioners' posts in favor of private sector talent. But Pappas believed that he needed technically trained specialists to run a modern city, and he felt that new faces would be harder to corrupt—at least in the short run. However, Pappas soon learned that everybody wanted to advise the mayor over dinner at Gracie Mansion, but nobody wished to surrender his lifestyle to serve New York. Events taught the mayor that the public had elected him to be its political gladiator. He stood all alone in the arena.

The mayor would recall arid recruiting efforts with graphic bitterness, whenever he suffered the isolation of high executive office.

"How's my favorite critic of the city hospital system?" the mayor delightedly asked Richard Simmon, chief of surgery at the elite New York Hospital.

"Good . . . just sewed another ventricle . . . Seven grand," the doctor responded with evident satisfaction.

"Forget the money. You can finally fix what's broken in this town, Mr. President of the Municipal Hospital Corporation." Mayor Pappas delivered the message as a gift bearer.

"You're jesting, of course," the doctor said with faint hope in his voice. After a pregnant pause, he continued, "There are better people for the job . . . I'll scout around."

The mayor grew more insistent. "I need you!"

"I'd love to . . . but I can't . . . the country house, the sports car . . . all belong to the bank. John, it's nothing personal," he said in a matter-of-fact way.

"It's nothing *but* personal when you abandon your city for a Porsche and a Hamptons cottage." Mayor Pappas hung up the phone, filled with disillusionment . . . and a little foreboding.

An undefeated Mayor Pappas dialed the Children's Welfare Alliance. Its energetic chairwoman, Norma Reid, combined a personal need to conquer new worlds with a deep belief that the broken welfare system could be made right. The mayor's friend had pioneered a successful low-cost curriculum that trained welfare mothers to meet their children's nutritional, medical, and educational needs from early infancy. Most importantly from the mayor's current perspective, she was not afraid of change; Norma Reid had taken the rare step of resigning from a life-tenured full professorship at NYU's Wagner School of Urban Affairs to lead the political fight for welfare reform. "The perfect candidate for Commissioner of Social Services," he thought.

After some personal words of thanks for her advice during the campaign, Mayor Pappas continued, ". . . and no more pressing our noses on the window pane. You call the shots at Social Services."

"You break my heart by giving me my

dream, John. I can still call you John, Mr. Mayor, can't I?"

"Don't even joke like that. We've been friends for fifteen years. What's with this heartbreak?" he said nervously.

"I earned my way through college, graduate school . . . you know, on the streets . . . got busted a few times. The press will destroy me when the background check is inevitably leaked. You know the kind of headline: 'Did Welfare Commissioner Practice What She's Preaching?'"

"I'll stick with you, come whatever," John said with iron commitment.

"I don't want to run the public gauntlet . . . and you can't afford the political capital. Let it go!" There was finality in her statement.

Mayor Pappas' body sunk in fatigue, accepting that his power was bound more by hypocritical convention than justice or common sense.

The mayor's next encounter was humiliating. He could overhear Tom Larson, senior litigating partner of prestigious Rice, Whitney & Patterson, whispering to the assembled lawyers and clients in his office that this was an important call from "his friend, the mayor," so please give him privacy.

"John, how can I help," was Larson's convention opener.

"As a matter of fact, I'm inviting you to be the city's general counsel."

"Great!" But it didn't sound so great the way Larson said it. "I can't just up and leave the firm. Anyway, I'm a private sector guy, the wrong man for a large bureaucracy, dogged by reporters, subject to eternal hearings. . ."

"Tom, I can't do it all by myself," the mayor was practically pleading.

"You don't understand. Someone like me grabs on to a shooting star when he's young and holds on for dear life. I latched onto Rice, Whitney at twenty-four, and I'm too afraid to let go at fifty. It would be a mistake," the litigator begged with fear in his cracking voice.

"I made the mistake," the mayor responded with simple finality.

Pappas began to appreciate the necessary convenience of relying on the permanent government provided by Frank Anselmo's "regulars." At the same time, he sought to balance his dependence on Anselmo by making the independent deputy mayor his confidante, protégé, and moral litmus test.

"What have you got?" the mayor inquired of his Deputy as they hurriedly crossed the City Hall Park grass to their revved-up vehicles.

"Shootout, Bushwick. Detective, dealer, six-year-old black kid caught in the crossfire."

"Go on . . ." the mayor pressed him.

"The kid's dead. And the dealer."

"The cop?" The Mayor was always deeply affected when a police went down in the line of duty.

"No good. Probably won't make it."

"Anything else?"

"The shooter was the nephew of mafia chieftain Paul Zapatti."

The mayor wearily dropped his head at the news. As they entered the vehicle, Calhoun turned to the Intel driver. "What's our ETA to Kings County Hospital?"

"We'll be there in twenty minutes," George replied in a military tone.

The mayor's black Lincoln sped out of City Hall's driveway, with two NYPD Intel officers tailing closely behind. George's colleague, Benny, radioed their ETA to the mayor's advance team at Kings County Hospital. Simultaneously with the vehicles' drivers sounding their sirens, both Benny and his counterpart in the back-up car reached out of the passenger side windows and attached magnetized red flashing lights to the roofs.

Mayor Pappas turned off the murder discussion, with a businesslike nod. "Okay, what are the calls?"

"Senator Marquand says the convention is coming here and you're set for the keynote," the deputy mayor reported.

"Set? No, they've penciled me in. Every promise in politics is written in very light pencil," he instructed.

The deputy mayor closed his eyes in not-so-mock reverie. "I see a big keynote. Thirty million Hispanic-Americans glued to their TV sets. You throw in a few down-home Spanish phrases. National ink. A new voice of empowerment. Cheering Latinos lining the barrios of San Antonio, Miami, and Los Angeles, all in search of a president with their own accent. And the Anglos will join because they also want to do what's right, if they think it wins and works. And you'll make it work."

Kevin spoke with the conviction that Pappas loved, although the mayor doused the fantasy with a little skepticism.

"Now that I'm elected president, what are your plans?"

"I'm going to keep stoking the dream no matter what you say," Kevin replied. "By the way, what happened with Anselmo out there?"

If you looked to your right or left at City Hall, it became clear that Deputy Mayor Calhoun was perceived to be from another planet. It was not so much his education at Harvard College and the Kennedy School of Government that separated him from the others at City Hall. It was him.

Calhoun was neither a liberal nor a conservative, catered to no one, and never sought or gave a quid pro quo for doing or getting what he thought was the right thing. Men like Anselmo were unpredictably predictable, because their erratic behavior could always be resolved into the common denominator of self-interest. Kevin, on the other hand, weighed each issue solely on its own merits, according to some self-defined mystical notion of the public interest. No one could count on him . . . so he was distrusted by everyone.

Elected officials feared Calhoun. He was not content to get their silent acquiescence on controversial issues. The deputy mayor exerted pressure to force legislators to openly agree to his policies, thereby exposing them to unnecessary political risks. He nurtured an ethical trickle-down theory that required the bureaucracy and citizens to observe that government business could be done transparently. But despite deep misgivings, elected officials had to deal with him, so long as the mayor let Kevin control the City's daily administrative apparatus. An elected official was a blind man without a cane if he couldn't access the bureaucratic agencies which delivered services and contracts to his constituency.

Mayor Pappas liked the fact that his deputy was smart, loyal, and a bit of a dreamer . . . and he wanted to be pushed by his deputy to challenge the system. It was also a dividend that everyone conveniently blamed Calhoun for the mayor's unwelcome displays of independence from the political machine. But Mayor Pappas knew that he could only push the organization so far before his government became ineffectual. In the end, he needed Anselmo's help to deliver the city and state legislatures on many controversial issues. And for re-election!

"We split the baby, with a bigger half for our point of view: Half the schools this year, half next . . . no frills," the Mayor said with satisfaction.

"Probably should have held something back. Anselmo will be back for more. He's a bottomless pit," offered Kevin.

"Bottomless or not, he's the party's state chairman. Two million registered voters in New York City. And he controls a couple dozen members of the City Council. You want to be effective for the people, so you learn not to piss up Anselmo's leg." There was no uncertainty in the mayor's view.

Calhoun felt equally sure that it was wrong to let Anselmo feed on the body politic, allowing him to get stronger and demand even more.

"We'd be better off trying to curb him instead of giving him more clout. Three years you've been giving in."

The mayor broke in: "You want me to spend four years in a procedural dogfight and at best end up in a standoff? There are real problems in this town. I'm elected to solve some of them, not to tilt with an abstraction." Mayor Pappas was talking so forcefully that it was clear he was telling his deputy to back off.

"I know Frank's your friend, but you've outgrown him. He's sleaze. Dirt inevitably rubs off."

"Sleaze or not, you'll have to work with him. There are a lot of talkers out there; we need Anselmo in order to *do*! And bottom line, Kevin, there is no power—and no dreams—if you're not reelected." It was clear that this subject of conversation was over, for now.

George turned to the mayor.

"ETA four minutes, sir."

Pappas leaned closer to Kevin.

"How old was the boy?" he asked in a whisper.

"Six."

"And what was our annual budget as of last night?"

"Thirty-five billion."

"New York sure spends a lot to kill its children," he uttered softly to no one in particular.

The mayor's shoulders dropped as his body slumped into the seat. His head limply fell to the headrest and his eyes closed in reflective sadness.

"ETA one minute, sir," George reported.

The Lincoln and its back-up rolled in almost perfect unity to a smooth stop at the curb of Kings County Hospital. Television strobe lights switched on to illuminate the gray space as cameramen hastily positioned themselves to capture the event.

About 200 mostly curious onlookers lined both sides of the entranceway, behind four-foot-high wooden police barricades. A tiny brown cluster burst into a chant, "Stop the genocide!" Lights and cameras swiveled to record the action and back again to Mayor Pappas emerging from his limousine.

As was customary, Deputy Mayor Calhoun preceded the mayor in leaving the vehicle and received a warm greeting from their advance man. TV journalists shouted, "Mr. Mayor, would you give us a comment on the shooting . . ."

Mayor Pappas responded, without breaking his quick stride, "Please, not now . . . There is no more painful moment for a mayor, than to visit a wounded police officer and his family."

As the mayor was whisked into the hospital through automatic sliding glass doors, he could hear an echo of his words rolling off reporters' lips with artificially pumped up excitement:

" 'There is no more painful moment . . .' These were the only words from a distressed Mayor Pappas, as he passed by angry black demonstrators . . . This is Bill-Susan-Dick-live from the scene at Kings County Hospital."

The cavernous block-long hospital hallway, elevator banks and corridors running off from it in every direction, was as always jammed with what seemed like a refugee evacuation in some undefined country. Multicomplexioned hordes speaking Creole, Yiddish, Spanish, Russian, Chinese, and, occasionally, English with a hard accent, moved quickly in no apparent order. A lone newsstand reinforced the foreign flavor with its Babel of linguistically varied publications, as did the people-clogged information booth bearing signs in all of these languages.

Human beings coughing, fevered, crippled, grief-stricken, drug-addicted, lost, determined, prayerful, resigned, hopeful, defiant, helpless . . . People just kept moving. Very few recognized Mayor Pappas and even those allowed him only a fleeting glance.

The advance man had arranged that an elevator be held for the mayor's party. They emerged on the third floor, which was packed tightly with police brass identifiable by their polished gold shields, tired homicide detectives held on duty from the 101st precinct night shift, Eddie Santos' family, and assorted hospital personnel.

Commissioner Coonan intercepted Mayor Pappas.

"What's it look like?" the mayor asked.

"Bad."

"Children?"

"A girl, five, and boy, three."

"What kind of departmental record?"

"Medal for Merit, Departmental Medal of Honor, never a sick day. Toughest cop in Brooklyn North," the commissioner hesitated to reflect his lack of comprehension.

"The wife, how is she?"

Commissioner Coonan looked in the direction of a small well-built, olive-skinned woman of about thirty-two, with two children clinging to her legs.

"You'll say hello, Elaine, Elaine Santos."

Kings County Hospital had hosted suffering and death since 1837. Bright posters could not relieve the dark, claustrophobic atmosphere that hung over its narrow hallways. This spiritually threatening aura caused police brass and others to huddle in groups in accordance with some primitive social instinct.

Mayor Pappas quietly shook Elaine Santos' hand. While pledging the city's support to her, he spontaneously lifted both children close to his body for a brief exchange of human warmth.

Across the corridor, Calhoun kept an eye on the mayor as the deputy mayor debriefed Detective Florian of the Internal Affairs Division Unit. Kevin observed an attractive young woman approaching the mayor and Mrs. Santos. A tall Irish girl, about twenty-nine, she appeared clever and tough, although she wore a wonderfully warm countenance. She was like a Gaelic twinkle wrapped in a fist.

"Who's the lady going up to introduce herself to Mrs. Santos and the mayor?" Calhoun inquired of Florian.

"She's one of us. A lawyer for the Detective's Endowment Association. I think her name is Marybeth Cogan. I was wondering how long it would take you to ask." Florian reveled in being ahead of anyone he talked to.

"Now you don't have to wonder anymore," Calhoun said with a smile. "What's her assignment?"

"In cases like these, the DEA assigns one of its investigators to protect the cop's reputation and pension rights." Florian's tone left the impression that nobody but he could find the answers, so all other investigatory efforts were by definition ridiculous.

"What happened?"

"I don't know yet." Florian was deliberately evasive. "Santos was meeting with a dangerous felon, without a 'ghost.' "

"What was the guy doing?" Calhoun knew that he would have to pry it out word by word from Florian.

"Meeting alone with a drug dealer? You got me. All I know is we got a dying cop, a dead kid, and a dead nephew of the head of the Zapatti family. Not too pretty." Florian's callous attitude contrasted so sharply with the image of Mayor Pappas holding the frightened Santos children that Calhoun felt chilled to the bone.

"Was Tino made?" Calhoun proceeded, despite his desire to abandon Florian.

"Are you kidding? A scumbag, a nothing. Too much of a hothead for the mob; a psychopath, who enjoyed other people's suffering for its own sake. Word is he had his uncle's ferocity without his self-control. A rap sheet this long." Florian spread his hands with two feet of air between them. "The punk belonged in Attica on a mandatory sentence. Instead he copped probation, which he recently skipped out on."

"Probation?" Calhoun's astonishment was evident.

"Isn't probation a stiff sentence in this town?" Florian replied mockingly to the civilian.

"The mayor's going to step up for the wife—"

Before Calhoun could elaborate, Florian fired a warning shot:

"I wouldn't if I were him."

Calhoun measured Florian in silence, as he continued: "Don't worry about it. We can bury Santos with his glowing reputation. Good cops turn bad, it happens all the time. And we give them an inspector's funeral to boot. Then a quiet investigation will tell us what really happened. It's too soon to put the mayor out on a public limb."

The metal doors from the operating room burst open, startling those assembled in the narrow corridor. A middle-aged nurse in a pale green, baggy uniform and puffy cap desperately tried to clear a path in front of Eddie Santos' stretcher, which was speedily propelled by four ICU nurses. "Give us room! Will you move! Move!" the nurses yelled.

A motionless Eddie Santos was enveloped by modern medical technology: Santos had a tube running down his trachea; a urinary catheter regulated his emissions; blood and vital fluids in dextrose solution flowed into his veins through intravenous tubes; and a heart monitor tolled his life. When the mayor and a gasping Mrs. Santos caught a glimpse of an inert Eddie Santos being propelled on the stretcher, Pappas shouted in his own distracted helplessness to Coonan, who stood right next to him: "For Chrissake, give these people some help."

Coonan instantaneously demonstrated that he had not forgotten his early experiences on traffic duty, as he effectively cleared a pathway for the ICU team.

The mayor, a priest, and Mrs. Santos were permitted into the ICU, along with two doctors and the head nurse. Suddenly the heart monitor erupted with a sickening, insistent sound alerting everyone to the flat line on its screen. The medical team launched an all-out effort to revive Eddie Santos' heartbeat. The nurse ripped off the cover sheet, exposing a long row of staples holding his sternum together. It had necessarily been cracked open to sew up the hole in his heart. A determined female doctor rhythmically pressed her palms deeply into Eddie's flesh in order to pump fresh blood into his still heart. This closed chest compression was immediately followed up by a male doctor at the head of the bed, who applied two large electric paddles to the sides of Santos' chest and zapped him in an effort to restart his heartbeat. The alternating compression and defibrillation techniques continued for fifteen minutes, until an exhausted doctor declared definitively, "We lost him."

The priest stepped forward and pulled a scarf from his pocket which he draped stole-like over his shoulders, while he removed anointing oil from his other pocket. He opened the vial and traced a cross on Santos' forehead with the side of his thumb. "Through His holy anointing may God, in His love and mercy give you the grace of the Holy Spirit."

Elaine was sobbing uncontrollably and Mayor Pappas gently embraced her. "We're with you, Elaine . . ." And looking at the Santos children's faces pressed against the ICU window, their eyes ladling out fear and confusion, the mayor continued: "The City takes care of its own."

Mayor Pappas stepped to Santos' bedside, made a silent prayer, and hurriedly exited the ICU, as the priest continued reciting: "May God, who frees you from sin, save you and raise you up."

CHAPTER FOUR

Paul Zapatti, sixty-nine year old don of the Zapatti family, strolled along the Coney Island boardwalk on his way to the borough president's retirement part at Gargivlos. His counselor and bodyguards followed watchfully in a black limousine at a respectful distance.

The five crime families had designated Zapatti to maintain their political and judicial connections in New York. The mafia commission understood that crime could be a dangerous business if it didn't have politicians and judges in its pocket. Even the high profit margins garnered from criminal enterprises did not make up for spending twenty years in prison. Knowing that money is permanent and power is transient—indeed, that money is an important element in obtaining and holding power—whenever possible the crime bosses willingly traded their bank accounts for protection by the powerful, so that they could continue business operations in relative security.

Zapatti recalled being at this very spot in Coney Island as a child, shoehorned in with hard-working immigrant families spending their day off at the beach; and at night the kids would be taken for rides on the spinning saucers, swirling airplanes, churning bumper cars, whooshing roller coaster, and soaring Ferris wheel, all topped off with Nathan's finest hotdogs, french fries and Good Humor bars. Today even Paul Zapatti was unsafe in most of Coney Island, where guns, drugs, and street gangs left only shuttered stands and motionless rusting metal. Zapatti gave an old man's nostalgic headshake at this carnage, but rationally he knew that the neighborhood's current residents were better customers for his business than their predecessors.

The mafia kingpin viewed himself as the quintessential capitalist, the soulless merchant who met demand in a consumer niche fueled by human weakness. Zapatti was like an insect who found a weakness in the human bark and burrowed in, sucking the vitality from his living victims. The defeated dulled their pain with his cocaine; the greedy or needy looked to Zapatti's loan sharks; the unloved played with his whores; and the bored thrilled to his gambling. Zapatti despised his customers. To him they were revolting creatures without respect for their families or themselves, leading short, chaotic lives of shameless violence toward each other and society. But sin was first and foremost the foundation of his non-cyclical business.

Sincerity, kindness, forgiveness, honor, warmth were not in Zapatti's dictionary. He was a loner, who spoke infrequently and usually sat impassively observing others around him. Zapatti decided fates and made business decisions based on his status, never stopping to explain his actions to anyone. His mob nickname was "Il Duro," the hard one, because of his uncompromising commitment to preserve the crime family at any cost. Human life or death meant nothing to Zapatti, apart from being instruments to achieve his goals. From time to time, New York's underworld would whisper that Il Duro murdered a disrespectful lieutenant with his own hands, in order to show that he was ultimately dependent on no one.

The dark clouds that precipitated the early

morning storm still hung over the city. When a sudden cloudburst caught Zapatti a few blocks from the restaurant, he didn't even look up; he continued to carry his baggy-suited 250-pound muscular frame with the short, determined steps of a conqueror who didn't acknowledge the elements. Before his driver could reach him, a feeble, wrinkled Sicilian of about the same age, who was a remnant of the old neighborhood, neatly dressed in a double breasted suit from at least thirty years ago, emerged silently from DeLuca's Fish Market and bowed respectfully. Without either of them speaking a word, the man opened his umbrella over Zapatti and walked faithfully behind him in the rain, a retainer in the procession of a medieval prince.

The long black limousine plowed down the street and jammed its brakes next to Zapatti. A sweating consigliere leaped from the still-moving car and ran towards his boss.

"Mr. Zapatti, Tino is dead! Shoot-out with a narc in the Carver projects. You better get off the streets."

Zapatti's eyes showed a momentary flash of pain and quickly reformed to onyx.

"We got the niggers selling in Bushwick. What the fuck was Tino doing up there?" were Zapatti's first words.

The counselor's expressionless face reflected

the emptiness of his heart. But fear of Zapatti created a permanent insecurity, just as it did with everyone else who dealt with him, because there was nothing more decent or glamorous about Paul Zapatti than any other serial killer. The silver-tongued courtroom counsel uncharacteristically stuttered, "Nobody knows, sir."

Once in the limo, Zapatti turned on the TV set for the local news. His picture appeared between those of Tino and Eddie Santos, with the reporter asking, "Is there a link?" He tuned it out with a quick click and spoke brusquely. "Find out what Tino was doing in Bushwick. Who put him up to it? And if the copy was dirty. This kind of trouble isn't good for anybody."

Carver Houses looked like Disneyland, with so many white men thrashing about. Zapatti's associates spotted their prey and screeched to a halt next to the fanciest pimp in Bushwick. As three well-dressed young men approached him, the dude droned in a monotous voice, "I told you guys, I saw nothing and know less. But I do know my constitutional rights."

Without a word, two of Zapatti's men arched his back over the hood of their car. The third sprung open a glinting twelve-inch stiletto and poked it into the soft flesh of the pimp's balls. With a childlike grin, the knife wielder uttered his first words: "Ya picked the wrong team, brother. We're from the dark side."

The pimp's voice crescendoed in recognition. "Don't slip, I use these things. I want to help you."

"Be quick! My hand is getting tired. Who was Tino with?" He pressed the blade a little deeper; the pimp's green trousers turned a soggy dark red with mushrooming blood stains.

"One of my girls knew Vinnie from the poolroom on Marcy. He came up to Tino, slapped him five, and ran like hell just as the shooting started. Martina hit the pavement, so she didn't see what happened."

"God bless, brother." The pimp was hurled to the sidewalk, exposing his shoulder holster.

"No quick moves, brother, or my friend will turn your head to dust." The wheel man made the threat credible by poking a sawed-off shotgun above the dashboard.

The crew reported immediately to Mr. Zapatti and he responded with a single phrase: "Find Vinnie!"

Vinnie circled mindlessly in the tiny safehouse room that his girlfriend had secured for him. He alternatively screamed, wept, and shook.

"I'm dead, Cookie. Only thing is whether my uncle or the cops get to me first."

"It was bad luck, we'll figure it out," his girlfriend said without conviction.

"You had to push. You said, one coke delivery, that's all we needed to get out of here. Boom! Crazy Eddie is in my face. I loved Tino, now he's dead. Now we're both dead!"

Cookie's dejection turned into defiance. "I was already dead, Vinnie. Shampooing heads that were always going someplace glamorous: Hobe Sound, Paris, East Hampton. And I knew where I was going—back to Brooklyn. Sam's Pizzeria, Doc's Bar, Joe's Bowling Alley, endless bullshit by the guys about heists, boosts, and rip-offs."

"What the fuck . . . You're young and beautiful. Those ugly bitches needed hair waxes, facials . . ."

Vinnie never understood how her mother's legacy influenced Cookie's vision of her future: alcohol, spreading hips, a pot belly, and long boring nights waiting for her husband to come home from his girlfriend's bed. Cookie feared her future of living hell more than death.

"Bullshit! How long before I start looking like my mother?" Cookie screamed.

"Longer than I got, baby!

Cookie mellowed and held the shivering youth.

"We'll find a way out, Vinnie. Don't worry, baby," she said softly.

"There's no way out of this one, babe," he replied desperately.

"There's always a way out!" Cookie finally said with an assurance which indicated some plan.

Mayor Pappas looked depressed as his limousine pulled away from the hospital.

"I better call Abe and tell him we'll be late for your speech to the Downtown Association luncheon," Calhoun said, waiting for some response.

"Sir, what's your pleasure," Calhoun tried again.

"My pleasure?" He skipped a beat in deep thought. "Where's the boy live?"

George picked up the radio. "Rainbow One to Rainbow Two. Give us a read on the dead boy's address."

"In the Carver Houses. Five-fifteen South Fifth Street," the radio crackled.

"Fifth Street, just off Broadway," George alerted the mayor.

"*That's* where we're going." Pappas was clear.

"We've got no advance man, no protection.

There could be a mob out there," Calhoun implored.

"I don't care who's out there. I want to do this. And we're going to. You know why? Because I'm the mayor."

"Rainbow Two, forget Downtown Association. Notify Abe to express apologies," George improvised.

Mayor Pappas had always been popular with minority constituents. But today he was greeted with a wall of silence and lowered heads, as he passed through thin clusters of neighbors standing in front of Bone's apartment building. He understood from his own upbringing that silence was the last redoubt of self-respect for the powerless. This community had made a collective judgment of shame against Mayor John Pappas, an empowered minority person who couldn't even protect their children from death delivered by the system that was supposed to nurture them.

As Pappas and Calhoun waded through the hallway stench and filth, the mayor absentmindedly expressed an unconscious childhood sentiment: "Terrible superintendent here."

Bone opened the door and stared impassively. His empty eyes reflected a man who no longer understood life and was existing only as a physical being. After a very long twenty seconds, Bone bowed slightly, saying in a tiny voice, "Your Honor," then executing a manne-quinlike turn into the small living room as the mayor followed him. In just one morning, old age had ambushed this young man. His taut stride had been replaced by the slow gait of life's victims.

At the sight of the father's sorrow, Mayor Pappas recognized that Bone had only memories of love left; no one to cry with, no one to touch; the mayor wanted to say, "I love you," but recognized it to be a hollow abstraction. John Pappas unconsciously wrapped his arms around a motionless Bone.

"It was a monstrous accident," Mayor Pappas whispered.

"Someone let the wolf out to eat my lamb. I want justice. I *will get* justice," Bone said.

As he left the apartment, Mayor Pappas felt the responsibility of the world on his shoulders. More specifically, the responsibility for Robby Bone's death.

CHAPTER FIVE

Walter Stern's sleek black Mercedes cruised past a screaming red sign "TOW AWAY: NO STANDING ANYTIME," mounted the sidewalk and parked at a forty-five degree angle behind the Brooklyn County Courthouse. His low license number spelled out Supreme Court Judge, privileged status for any non-local traffic enforcement officer who might not know the vehicle itself.

Judge Stern's deliberate demeanor and appearance bespoke who he was: a battered forty-year-old briefcase exited the car first; Stern's ritualistic black Brooks Brothers' cashmere overcoat, on top of his habitual dark blue woolen Sulka suit, custom-made Charvet white shirt, and understated red Hermes tie showed themselves next; and finally came his pale, slightly fleshy face, rimless wire spectacles and full head of wavy white hair. This perfect image of what a judge should be was hardly a career jurist. In fact, Stern was, until recently, the patrician senior partner of a 500-lawyer Wall Street firm. To the astonishment of the legal establishment, Stern wanted to cap his career with local public service to the city he loved. He had been endorsed enthusiastically by Mayor Pappas who recommended him to Frank Anselmo. It was the party boss who actually dictated judicial nominations and elections of Supreme Court judges through a pro forma judicial selection convention controlled by local political clubhouses, followed by vote-pulling of regulars on typically low turn out, off-year judicial election days. After two years of service Stern had already earned a reputation as a tough but fair judge, although some thought he was a little too intellectual, too much in the Yale Law School tradition, for the local bench.

Judge Stern joined other employees returning from lunch on the steep climb up the stone steps in front of the Federal-style courthouse. As he approached the entrance, Stern observed a gaggle of reporters and TV cameras encircling a lone black man standing catatonically still in a sunless corner. In the center of the circle was a grim-faced Edgar Bone. Bone excited orgasms in reporters, used to watching people moon for their TV cameras, by not speaking a single syllable into their thirsty microphones. Bone's charcoal-black mourning suit was adorned solely by his silver star from Vietnam. And his dead face was framed for the TV cameras against a hand printed sign featuring a biblical injunction: "JUSTICE, JUSTICE. YOU ARE TO PURSUE JUSTICE." A photograph of Bone's murdered son was stapled beneath the lines from Deuteronomy, as a stinging indictment of an unnamed defendant.

Bone had visions of Robby's small ghost leading him by the hand to save other children through cleansing the system. Having nothing more to lose, Bone became the most dangerous kind of enemy with an untameable obsession to bring down the system that murdered his boy. Justice would be the only fitting monument to his son. Bone took the ancient Christian approach of standing silent witness, until he broke the conscience of the man who let out the wolf to eat his lamb. Like Ghandi's passive resistance strategy to liberate India from the British, it would only work if Bone had a moral enemy; unknowingly, in Judge Walter Stern, the enemy was a decent man.

This one-on-one biblical trial of a judge presented a banquet to New York's hungry media.

As Stern climbed the steps, he was shocked to see the much-respected former Mayor Ed Koch doing his Fox News political commentary live from the courthouse steps:

"One distraught father's unconquerable commitment to justice poses such a direct challenge to the system that there is no way to ignore it. If the judges cannot protect our children, who is left? They are the final port of independence in a turbulent democracy, whether you are a little guy or a big guy. Judge Walter Stern failed us! He must explain why he paroled a mafia-connected, psychopathic drug dealer to kill a child and a hero detective. One simple man, Edgar Bone, demands to know the truth for all of us."

Judge Stern saw his life and career pass in front of him. Stern knew that from this moment on, he no longer held the key to his own destiny. It was confirmed when a clutch of reporters spotted the judge, unexpectedly surrounded him at the entrance while screaming questions he could only partially hear in the bedlam: "Tino Zapatti . . . sweetheart sentence . . . probation report . . . mafia influence . . ."

Judge Stern could not break through the frenzied reporters. He circled frantically trying to find an escape route, a fox trapped by bloodthirsty hounds. All the while he repeatedly shouted, "No comment . . . please . . . no comment . . . what's going on here?"

Peter Ragan, the judge's forty-year-old devoted law clerk was alerted to the pandemonium as he waited in the hallway to join Judge Stern at a hearing. He recruited a phalanx of court officers who, with a determined charge, freed the judge from his tormentors.

Bone observed the judge's ordeal without even blinking. The words "justice, justice" hung leadenly in the air, like a tropical humidity. Court officers blocked the pack, while a frazzled Judge Stern fled into an elevator with Ragan.

"Get me the Zapatti probation file." were his only words as the judge stood shaking with his back against the elevator wall.

CHAPTER SIX

The press office scheduled a mayoral press conference in the Blue Room at three PM. This way, City Hall could feed the official story of what was now euphemistically called by its shorthand name the "Carver incident" to the broadcast journalists for the six o'clock news shows and to the print reporters before their four PM deadlines. Abe Bauman, the mayor's chief of staff who controlled internal administration at City Hall, was carefully orchestrating the event.

The Blue Room was in fact powder blue, with white ornamental trim running fully around the space at waist- and near-ceiling-levels. Its finest touches were three floor-to-ceiling windows which looked out over City Hall Park and its relatively intact 1920s skyline, including such architectural monuments, now grade B office space, as the Woolworth and old AT&T buildings.

The Blue Room looked large and dignified empty, but once it was filled with five rows of chairs occupied by reporters, a ten-foot-wide wooden platform cluttered with six TV cameras and cameramen, plus lights and wires running in every direction, and dozens of political retainers lined three deep against every inch of side wall space, it seemed very small and antiquated, and it was always stuffy-hot, whatever the season of the year.

Abe communicated by hand-held radio on an open frequency to the mayor's car and got its ETA.

"Two minutes! Two minutes! Heads up!" he shouted in alert.

Still photographers loaded film and readied their shutters. Reporters put away cellulars and took out notebooks, while several others agilely balanced tape recorders on their knees.

Abe also informed Calhoun of Bone's vigil on the courthouse steps and the incredible media attention that it was already receiving. Calhoun switched on the TV in the car and they watched in silence.

"It's pretty rough coverage," Kevin finally said. I've never seen anything like this. The story is so bizarre—the innocent kid, the war-hero father, the superhero undercover cop, the bleeding heart judge, the convicted drug scum walking the streets on probation, and the god-damn Godfather, Paul Zapatti himself, sitting on top of the whole thing like a cherry on the sundae."

Mayor Pappas shook his head in resignation and took a slug of his scotch.

"I've asked a friend to see if anyone is advis-ing Bone," Calhoun continued. "You look at him, you look at those totally empty eyes, and you'd think maybe he's a little nuts. But you look at the coverage he's getting with this 'bearing witness' business, makes you wonder if he hasn't got some Republican PR guru whispering in his ear. I mean, did you see Stern's face? It looked like he had seen a ghost."

"Or some avenging angel," Pappas replied.

"Yeah, whatever," Kevin mumbled. "It shows Bone knows what the marchers haven't learned—that less is more. He just stands and stares and they can't get enough of him. They stick microphones in his face and he keeps his mouth shut. No reporter has ever met anyone who can resist blabbing into a microphone, so naturally they're hysterical about this 'biblical' phenomenon."

"Nobody's telling him what to do," Pappas said softly. "You've been hanging out with politicians too long, Kevin. We're the ones who wait for our Madison Avenue advisers to tell us how to convey the emotions we want the people to think we're feeling. But some people, even some ordinary, common people, when they're ravaged by grief, can just instinctively do something dramatic, something, I don't know, majestic. There's a desperate need to fill the emotional void with a purpose.

"You're too young to understand deep suffering. It's like no other pain to lose a son; it's the roughest," Pappas said, lost in his own thoughts. "You see Bone on the television, he looks like a dead man himself standing there keeping his vigil. But he isn't dead. He's only ravaged. I've been ravaged, Kevin. At least dead is over. Dead doesn't hurt. Burying a son will ravage you, Kevin. I know exactly how Mr. Bone feels. Exactly! When they flew my boy home from Vietnam, with all the salutes and honor guards and folded flags and watching everybody cry when they play 'Taps' every time you turn around, when that happened I was ravaged."

Kevin had never seen Pappas like this: completely still, almost frozen, words pouring out of lips that didn't seem to move. "At least I could tell myself that Johnny died for a purpose. An ambiguous purpose . . . an increasingly ambiguous purpose . . . but at least some kind of purpose. But what can Mr. Bone tell himself? Why did his Robby die?" Suddenly the mayor seemed to come back to life. His chest swelled and he spit out his words as if they were on fire. "Robby Bone died because he had the gall, because he had the temerity to think that he could walk to school along a street in the rain at eight o'clock in the morning in New York City."

Pappas halted for a moment.

"The question we have to answer, Kevin, isn't what Mr. Bone can tell himself. It's what can I tell Mr. Bone. And what can I tell the people of New York? Finally, what can I tell myself? I'm in charge of the city that killed Robby Bone."

Kevin desperately tried to think of something he could say that would ease the pain his mentor felt.

"I'm sorry, Kevin," Pappas said, his voice and his emotions once again under control. "Those were rhetorical questions. No need to answer them. No answers anyway. But thanks for trying. And thanks for listening. I was just thinking out loud, trying out some ideas for the child's eulogy tomorrow."

Abe escorted a group of black ministers from Brooklyn into the Blue Room and they formed a small semi-circle several feet back from the podium. A black reporter from *The Sun* turned to a colleague in the next chair and nodding in the direction of the clerics he said, "Lining up the ducks," in apparent reference to the mayor's attempt to show support in the minority community for his handling of the Carver incident.

"Thirty seconds," announced Abe.

Plainclothesmen swung open the doors to City Hall as the mayor, Deputy Mayor Calhoun at his side, hustled up the steps and into the rotunda. Leslie Christos, the mayor's press secretary appeared at his shoulder as he kept moving down the narrow west corridor, through the low iron and brass gate manned by Intel guarding the mayor's end of the hall.

"Who's up?" the Mayor asked Leslie.

"*The Post*"

"Sadler, or Marx?"

"Sadler," she sounded a little frustrated.

"I know what's coming. 'Is probation a sentence in this town?'" the mayor offered from previous encounters.

Leslie was prepared for this question and read from her notes: "Judge Stern has a powerful record on the bench. He has served two years and meted out some of the stiffest punishments in the city. If the report he received from Leonard Street recommends 'probation,' then probation it has to be! After that they'll start on the mandatory crap."

"I got it, I got it," he replied with the impatience of a star waiting to go on stage.

From inside the Blue Room he could hear Abe yell "Lights," and the place came ablaze with electrical and human intensity at the mayor's entrance. News photographers leaped forward, flashbulbs erupted, the clerics blinked at the blinding lights; the TV cameras rolled as the cameramen on the platform communicated by hand signals with the reporters who called the shots from their chairs up front.

Abe's and Calhoun's eyes locked. The former jerked his head toward the door and Calhoun responded with two fingers—in effect, "Give me two minutes"—and positioned himself in a corner where he could observe the whole room.

The mayor stepped up on the stage, shook hands with the ministers, and embraced the last one. A photographer yelled, "Beside them!" and Mayor Pappas, after glancing over at Leslie and receiving affirmation, posed for the photo opportunity. Finally, the mayor stepped up to the podium, began to unfold a written statement, and then impulsively returned the sheet to his jacket pocket.

The Mayor spoke extemporaneously. "Good morning. I would like to welcome the Reverend Williams and Reverend Birch from the Abyssinian Baptist, the Reverend Spellman from AME Zion, and my dear friend, Reverend Milton Parks of the First Church of Harlem. Thank you, reverend gentlemen, for having the courage to stand here beside me."

Calhoun was satisfied with the staging of the proceedings and signaled Abe that he was ready for their meeting. Each of them unobtrusively slipped out of different side doors in the Blue Room, independently proceeding through the mayor's alcove, where all of the secretaries and police were glued to the city-owned Channel 31 watching a live broadcast of Mayor Pappas' press conference. They finally met behind a closed door in the deputy mayor's office.

Kevin switched on Channel 31, as he examined sheets of paper bound in a file marked "Probation Department."

"Where's the probation report?" Kevin asked as he handed the records back to Abe. Abe reached familiarly into the file, plucked out a completed form, and handed it to the Deputy Mayor.

"Looks okay," Calhoun commented with admitted lack of knowledge in his voice.

"Very okay. But there is a conviction. Criminal possession in the fourth degree," Abe observed.

"4-C is a probational offense. So what's the problem?"

"Kevin, there are 4-C's and there are 4-C's," Abe responded while checking over the details of the report.

"You keep looking at that as if it were not kosher," Kevin said inquiringly.

Now kosher was something Abe knew about, even more than probation reports, since he had spent a lifetime as an Orthodox Jew and only sixteen years in the civil service including his two-year stint in the probation department.

"A cut of meat is kosher. A piece of fruit is kosher. Savory foods and all kinds of dainties are kosher. But this probation report is not kosher." Abe's Talmudic discourse clearly left the impression that something was wrong with the report, so Kevin demanded, "Just give it to me straight. What's wrong with that report?"

"*Too* kosher," was Abe's simple response.

"Translation?"

"The virgin looks pregnant to me," Abe indicated in a scholarly intonation, as he bent over the document. "You see here, the supervisor signed this."

"So?" Kevin waited for the payoff.

"That's a lot of weight for a 4-C. What happened to the original little probation officer, where's his signature?"

Calhoun grabbed the report, trying to understand the full importance of the observation.

"Surely there must be an explanation."

"The more flesh, the more worms," Abe responded coolly with a Talmudic quote.

Meanwhile on the TV in the background the mayor was completing his press conference, with a pledge that the City would leave no stone unturned in its investigation. "These murders are already known as 'The Carver Incident.' But I'm telling you this is an incident that will not go away, not as long as I am mayor of this city. In the whole city, in all parts of the city, Bushwick and Greenpoint, Jamaica and Harlem, Washington Heights and Brownsville, the bodies drop, shot like fish in a barrel, and the accusation is we don't care because these are disenfranchised parts of the city. Homicide is homicide whether it's on Park Avenue or up an alley in Williamsburg, and we will find the perpetrators and we will put them away. Whose bullet killed the child, you're going to ask? We'll find out. Important, but more to the point we're addressing here, who's going to give Eddie Santos back to his wife and children? And Robby Bone back to his father? Questions?"

Calhoun measured Abe and abruptly muted the TV. "I think this report calls for a visit to the probation department."

CHAPTER SEVEN

It was rare for a policy-maker at City Hall to visit the 180,000 bureaucrats he administered in the sprawling complex of municipal buildings, courthouses, detention centers, and computer facilities around City Hall Plaza and their satellites in each borough. Communications between City Hall's policy-makers and the bureaucracy occurred via the media or by specific directives to commissioners; City Hall's policy changes might cause the civil servants to shift slightly to the right or left, be somewhat tighter or looser on fiscal matters, or be tougher or more lenient in enforcement. For the most part, however, New York City's civil service functioned autonomously.

As the deputy mayor left his office with Abe, he grabbed an envelope containing architectural renderings.

"If we're walking by Chambers Street, I ought to stop by the building department," he said with some annoyance. "For some reason, engineering plans are not being delivered to city construction sites on a timely basis." Calhoun waved the envelope to emphasize the apparent simplicity of delivering it. "The delay is costing the City one million dollars a day."

"Has OMB pinpointed the bottleneck?" Abe inquired with the sobriety of a veteran who had experienced this sort of thing many times before.

"The geniuses in the Office of Management and Budget narrowed it down to the building examiner's office. Now to get it fixed," he replied with skeptical determination. "And then we're off to Leonard Street to learn why Tino Zapatti walked." It was clear from his emphasis that the deputy mayor's priority rested with the latter.

Kevin and Abe looked like tennis spectators, trying to cross Chambers Street, as 200 cars per minute poured westward onto it from the Brooklyn Bridge and hundreds more aggressively pushed eastward to nearby Wall Street or the FDR uptown ramp. Abe's and Kevin's brisk pace and serious attitude indicated that they were concerned with weighty matters, but the thousands of cars carrying ordinary people in every direction on routine daily business seemed to diminish the impression that the citizens' lives depended on the outcome of the Calhoun-Bauman mission.

The twenty-nine story Municipal Building was a venerable cathedral to the bureaucracy. Calhoun and Abe hurried down a block-long unadorned corridor, punctuated by scratched wooden doors on both sides of the hallway. The doors sported signs of obscure agencies. They stopped at a door marked BUILDING EXAMINER. A long line of bored "expediters" stretched down the corridor. It moved so slowly that unattended briefcases could hold their places for long periods without being moved. The building code and its administration was so complex and daunting that businessmen, indeed even ordinary citizens, had to hire politically connected "expediters" to get routine approvals. Since time was money in construction, as mortgage interest on land had to be paid whether one was building or waiting for permission to start, approvals could spell life or death. Middlemen were able to safely grease compromised bureaucrats and the political machine with hidden gratuities and legal campaign contributions at Anselmo's political dinners.

Abe and Calhoun entered into a cramped two-person office, inhabited by four middle-aged women. Edna, wearing a smock and brown tortoise-framed glasses, sat behind her desk with envelopes neatly piled high around her, except for a neatly carved-out space in the center of her desk, which was occupied by a tea mug engraved with her name and covered with smile stickers.

"It's the deputy mayor. I gotta hang up," she said excitedly into the phone. "What are you doing here?"

Calhoun spread out the blueprints on the small unoccupied floor space and, pointing to the drawings, he asked the four women evenly, "Why aren't these prints getting to the job site on a daily basis?"

"Daily? Every day? I can't," Edna said in a shaken voice.

"What do you mean, you can't? The delay is costing the city over a million dollars a day," Calhoun replied more in puzzlement than anger.

"I can't because I don't have enough of the big envelopes and I can't fold the prints into the smaller envelopes because the engineers say they can't read on the crease." Edna seemed pleased to be able to share her dilemma with higher authority.

"Why don't you have enough big envelopes?" Calhoun was doggedly on the trail.

"Her! She's got all the big envelopes and I'll be damned if I'm going to keep going over and begging her for them," Edna glanced over her shoulder with a frown.

"What? Who?" Kevin was dumbstruck.

"Her. Tessie. Back there. She wants us all to beg her for the big envelopes. Who put her in charge of everything?" she shouted spitefully.

Calhoun, followed by Abe, walked over to Tessie.

"Don't listen to her. They cut the big envelopes out of the last budget. They said we didn't need big envelopes because the City wasn't building anything big anymore," Tessie threw out as an absolute defense.

"I know. I sympathize. But where are the remaining big envelopes?" He forced himself to progressively soften his tone in order to gently lead her along.

"They're in the back, but she won't take them for spite," Tessie said and then she whispered to the deputy mayor, "She's very spiteful. She won't even let us use her plug to make hot water." Tessie waved a pot. "See? We've got to go to the ladies' room to boil water. Is that fair?"

Tessie was seeking justice, but Calhoun only wanted to reverse the City's one-million-dollars per day loss.

Calhoun smiled in agreement, picked up two boxes of the large envelopes and started back toward Edna's desk.

"Is it? Just because she sits near the electric outlet, that makes it hers?" Tessie had grown more agitated with the sight of Calhoun moving the envelopes.

Deputy Mayor Calhoun plunked the envelopes on Edna's desk, and handed her his card with a firm command: "Here. From now I want the plans delivered every day. Understand? If you run out of envelopes call Abe." Abe dutifully gave her his business card.

"Sure, but I don't want them using this socket. They leave their junk all over my desk. Sugar, crumbs. They think I'm their maid." Edna gave the deputy mayor a firm handshake, holding his hand between her warm palms, and then, with her right hand raised, solemnly repeated an oath after Calhoun, to deliver the plans daily. Then Abe and Calhoun moved on to the probation office to investigate the Carver murders.

Civil servants were hired for life based on test scores; however, 20,000 "provisional" positions, often the highest-paying slots, were carved out as requiring "temporary specialized skills," for which no tests were necessary. These coveted positions were generally filled with politically active members of Anselmo's clubhouse system or City Hall loyalists. And "temporary" usually become forever with provisional appointees, unless they lost their political rabbi. Furthermore, promotions and merit pay for the entire civil service system depended on supervisory evaluations and sometimes support from politically connected supervisors, who themselves were often beholden to Anselmo for their advances.

The probation department building on Leonard Street was relatively new by city standards; however, the deferred maintenance inside already gave it that unloved, decadent look.

"His name is Schwartz," Abe briefed Calhoun.

Larry Schwartz, career civil servant and Director of the Probation Department, was a combat veteran of many political and civil service wars.

"A *lantsman* of yours?"

"*Lantsman, lantsman,*" Abe corrected his accent. "Stop trying your Yiddish out on me with a Shakespearean accent."

"Okay, okay, do you know him?

"Sure. But I was long gone from the department when the Zapatti case came up, and I wouldn't know any of the junior officers."

Abe and Calhoun passed through a hive of desks, clearly gaining the curious attention of the drones. Kevin was spiritually disheartened making his way through the probation department, feeling much as he did as a child when his father preached about dead civilizations, dead people, and the hopeless condition of man. Had he visited, Dante would have chiseled *The Inferno's* signature warning, "Abandon all hope, ye who enter these gates," on Leonard Street's façade.

The deputy mayor couldn't figure out whether the sullen parolees or the probation officers who looked worn-out by their permanent states of depression were the more hopeless. Both appeared to lead lives that were pointless jokes, separated only by being seated on opposite sides of the same desks. Politicians unable to find money in their budgets to build enough jail cells perpetuated the myth of rehabilitating prisoners prematurely released on parole to make space for new ones; of course, they didn't supply the funds or skilled personnel to give any substance to their pretense. Parolees and probation officers were joined by political default at the hip, in a cycle of arrest, probation, crime, re-arrest, probation . . . Kevin could not help feeling sorry for these people who were forced to spend a lifetime going through ritualistic motions that predictably must amount to nothing.

Calhoun and Bauman finally came upon a glassed-in office space wearing the gold stenciled name of its occupant, Larry Schwartz. As Calhoun and Abe entered, the supervisor came to a somewhat staged noisy and scraping attention.

The slight, wiry, bald-headed director was not happy to see his visitors.

"Please . . ." Calhoun motioned for him to be seated.

"You're the first deputy mayor to set foot on this floor. We had a commissioner once, but he was on the wrong floor," Schwartz noted with a touch of "so what are you doing here; it can't be good for me" in his voice. None of them had yet taken the initiative to be seated, so Calhoun broke the ice.

"May I have a seat?"

"Of course. And Abe, you're at home already."

"Hello, Larry." There was no joy in Abe's greeting. And they all sat down.

"I know why you're here," Schwartz volunteered. I've logged twelve calls already today. Mr. Zapatti. . . ?"

"Yes," Calhoun replied.

"Why did he have to be my case?" he said anticipating the deputy mayor's questions.

"Exactly!"

"Because sometimes we get overloaded," Schwartz indicated with a shrug.

"And you take the extras?" Calhoun finished Schwartz's thoughts with a question.

"The extra-specials."

"Such as a Zapatti family member?" The deputy mayor sounded sarcastic.

"Something like that. Look, Mr. Deputy Mayor . . ." Schwartz was fed up with being baited.

"Kevin's good enough," Calhoun offered in such a way that his preferred informality increased the hierarchical tension.

"Any case comes in here that looks like it's 'connected,' I take a special interest in. To avoid making mistakes," Schwartz explained.

Kevin jumped on Schwartz's vague explanation with a sharpness that evidenced his dissatisfaction.

"You made one on this one," Calhoun said raising the confrontational stakes.

"And for that, I'm extremely sorry. I've written letters of condolence to Mr. Bone and Mrs. Santos—we're advised not to do such things—litigation—but I don't give a shit. I blew one and I don't mind admitting it. But I'd rather blow one out of a hundred, then send ten men away on mandatories who don't deserve them." Schwartz retreated into bureaucratic mumbo-jumbo to duck the inquest.

"You sound like an enlightened man, Mr. Schwartz," Kevin said scornfully.

"And you sound like you're fucking with me. You got anything to add Abe?" Schwartz verbally separated out Kevin as an enemy, indicating an end to even their polite sparring.

"No, Larry, you're doing fine," Abe said communicating the understanding of one veteran to another, but without giving Schwartz any comfort.

"Everybody's going to want to know how these things happen," Calhoun said by way of seeking an explanation which at least made sense to himself.

"How long have you been on this job, Kevin?" Schwartz delivered the question as a message from a combat-hardened professional to an ROTC officer.

"Three years."

"And you're looking to go to the Oval Office soon?"

"You're also an acute observer of the political scene," Calhoun said with a smile.

"These things happen because we're awash in criminals, in half-baked social workers, in a city that doesn't function, in a world that doesn't know right from wrong," Schwartz informed the novice, with the subcontext of "stop riding my back for the sake of Mayor Pappas' political ambitions."

"That's why I got out of here," Abe said, focusing on the facts alone.

"You escaped just in time," Schwartz murmured longingly.

Calhoun rose from his chair and held out his hand to the supervisor, and said, "Mr. Schwartz," before he was interrupted by Schwartz turning down the confrontational atmosphere with an informality, which was being used to demarcate a truce rather than to indicate that either believed the war was over.

"Larry."

"I owe you an apology, I came here with a big head of steam and . . ."

Calhoun was again cut off, as both sides temporarily tried to achieve a gracious disengagement.

"No apologies. It takes more than three years to get up to speed in this department. There's only one man who would have made a good probation officer: Kafka. And he wasn't available," Schwartz's irony seemed real, as he emphasized the absurdity of his job as much to himself as to the deputy mayor.

Calhoun nodded and started his departure with a smile.

"Give me a call, Abe, and if anything opens

up in the big building, keep me in mind," Schwartz said knowing that these words were an empty hope.

After the door closed, Schwartz fell into his chair because he recognized that Calhoun was a formidable opponent. He had so far just survived the first round.

CHAPTER EIGHT

Magazines referred to Lenny Lasker as the "billionaire tycoon," although he hardly had any equity. Lasker was a real estate glutton. As soon as a project was completed or even became familiar to him, Lenny abandoned it to subordinates while he restlessly moved to the edge of a new precipice. He had a black hole in his soul which could be filled only momentarily by gambling everything, and then some more, on the next big deal. Beating someone out of his due, rather than success itself was Lenny's emotional currency.

Long ago Lasker stopped caring about people, if he ever had; he breathed real estate but his obsession was not so much with building as with deals, numbers, mortgages, and ultimately money. Lasker had no friends, only connections. Connections were people who could be bribed, flattered, or frightened into doing his bidding. Enemies were those who were actual or potential obstacles to his will, precisely because they could not be bribed, flattered, or frightened. Other people were irrelevant because they couldn't add to or subtract from his empire. His family fit into the latter category. He treated his young third wife like chattel after forcing her to sign an ironclad prenuptial agreement, and he degraded his children until they fit his preconceived image of dependent pilot fish.

Lasker wanted respect, but received only flattery. Socialites and charities wooed him for donations and businessmen kissed his ass for contracts, but Lenny was never invited to serve on a single corporate or charitable board of directors or asked to join any social club. Thus, he had a relentless hate and envy of the establishment and was left only to lord financial dominance over it. When a critic accused Lasker of being a monster, he always defended himself in the same way: "I've built fifteen million square feet of office space in New York. What have you done with your life?" And he would walk off before getting an answer.

Across the narrow East River, a wall of magnificent skyscrapers and luxury apartment buildings stared arrogantly down on the deserted landscape of Long Island City. The Manhattan skyline seemed to be embarrassed by its once proud sister, whose only link to a glorious past was that she pretentiously clung to her now fictitious designation as an independent city.

Lasker's strange entourage of one stretch and two baby limousines roared across the Queensboro Bridge, made a sharp right turn, and began to plow up the ancient cobblestones that precariously covered the twisting streets of Long Island City. They indifferently passed squalid factories that once housed the best of nineteenth century industry: America bought its pencils, paper clips, staples, wire, chewing gum, leather goods, and light bulbs from these now forgotten warehouses. And its crumbling piers, reputed to be the finest to ever receive clipper ships, were once covered with the world's raw materials. Long Island City was left with only two assets: hundreds of tiny sweatshops employing thousands of mostly female Hispanic immigrants and spectacular views of Manhattan's gold coast. Lasker was here to get rid of the former, in order to exploit the latter.

Lenny had already assembled enough waterfront land to construct a 1.5 million square foot office tower for BancExchange, a giant out-of-state financial conglomerate which planned to relocate 3,000 jobs in Long Island City. But this was not enough for Lasker. He fumed over the turndown that his purchase offer received from Meyer & Son, a decrepit garment factory whose destruction would allow Lenny to build an additional 500,000 square feet. Lasker salivated over the possibility of leasing space at high rents to law firms, accountants, brokers, and others who did, or desired to do, business with BancExchange.

The limousines chewed up Vernon Boulevard and then made a right turn onto Forty-fourth Drive. Manhattan burst into their vision. From the desolate wharves of Long Island City, Manhattan was reborn a virgin each dawn. Lasker took notice of his environment for the first time. His eyes danced excitedly from the assertive sparkle across the river to the enervating decadence around him. And his whole body lusted for this deal!

Lasker's caravan surprised a youthful construction worker standing at ease in the middle of Van Dam Street. Upon awakening to its presence, he began to furiously wave his red caution flag. The procession halted about fifty feet from its destination, a red-bricked loft building with a faded hand painted sign:

"MEYER & SON, EST, 1939." A huge crane, with a bold insignia stenciled on its side—"NEW YORK WATER AUTHORITY"—was hoisting an ancient section of water main from its trenched crypt.

The travelers dismounted. Lasker glanced at Meyer's loft and mumbled, "What a waste." His two bodyguards lined up in tight formation on either side of him, while his lawyer and PR man walked in step behind them. Many wealthier and more venerable New Yorkers navigated the City's streets alone. Lasker's torpedoes were there for his ego gratification rather than for physical security. Lenny Lasker, the geek of Roosevelt High School, could finally afford to buy his own gang.

His lawyer and flack made potential opponents cringe, because Lenny's hostility had no limits. Irrespective of the provocation Lenny always fought to the death, if his opponent was weaker. The flack viciously smeared adversaries in the press, while the litigator bled them into financial ruin with frivolous lawsuits. Although Lenny was immaculately dressed as always, his banker's blue suit could not hide the vulgarity and brutality which bulged beneath every seam.

Lasker displayed his first smile of the day at the sight of this usually desolate street ablaze with flashing lights turning atop police cars, fire trucks, and assorted city emergency vehicles. City revenue agents and overweight political hacks in blue jumpsuits, emblazoned with bold block white letters—"CITY MARSHAL"—carried boxes of documents out of the factory doors.

A sanitation inspector in a crisp green uniform with gold braid calmly wrote a $500 violation, as nearly hysterical workers used a mixture of Spanish and English in a futile attempt to dissuade him.

"We've been stacking these bags eight years, nobody says nuthin'. All of a sudden, twice a day, like clockwork, you're here," shouted an enraged worker flailing the air with hands shrouded in thick elbow-length rubber gloves.

"Simple! City code states it is unlawful to leave garbage in the street," said the inspector, never lifting his eyes or pen from the summons.

"The industrial carters won't pick up unless the bags are in the street," another frustrated worker screamed in anger at the obvious.

"The law is the law," the inspector replied in carefully controlled tones. And with total banality he handed over the ticket.

A long line of yoked female prisoners with thick rope tied around their wrists and between their palms, then running to the next link in this human chain, stretched from the factory door to waiting immigration vans. The ordeals of life had provided these victims with natural anesthesia for its disasters. It was impossible to read any emotion in their gentle, brown faces, which resignedly wore the masks of the damned. They had long ago been sentenced to a twelve-hour workday at dingy factories, earning enough to cover minimal personal living costs and to send money to somebody they loved: elderly parents or hungry children in some distant Latin country they called home. The breadwinners' deportations meant unfathomable hardships for many unseen faces.

The senior immigration officer approached Lenny at the entrance to the factory.

"Good morning Mr. Lasker," he nodded warmly.

Lasker looked down at his gold-and-silver linked Cartier watch.

"Not even seven AM and you guys are already doing a hell of a job. Civil servants sure get a bum rap," he said with an admiring pat on the back.

"We do what needs to be done," the inspector responded matter-of-factly. And in the same breath he started shouting commands to his men: "Load them up! We haven't got all day." He sounded more like a commissar than a public servant.

Lasker was so eager that he practically ran into the ramshackle factory. Vats of dye emulsified in their idleness and giant bolts of white cloth stood motionless, totems witnessing a cruel spectacle. City inspectors were deploying the most lethal weapons of modern bureaucratic warfare to destroy Meyer's factory: health inspectors searched for Legionnaires' disease in the dismantled ventilation system; fire officers scanned every inch of the sprinkler system with laser devices so sensitive that they could uncover microscopic leaks; and surgically masked building department inspectors dressed in white, chemically treated canvas suits and boots gleefully ripped and tossed asbestos from the loft's tall ceiling.

The 150 workers who survived the immigration purge sat in demoralized silence behind their lifeless machines. Resistance was useless; their fates were sealed. They exchanged sorrowful glances or furtively hurled curses with their eyes at the uniformed terrorists.

Lasker pushed his way through the stir, toward a glass-enclosed rectangular office at the end of the factory floor. Its transparency left no room for concealment. Ben Meyer and his son rose abruptly from behind their scarred desks, which had stood opposite each other for forty-two years.

Upon sensing the challenge, Lenny's eyes tensed into menacing slits. His pace quickened. Old man Meyer bolted from the office with the agility of a much younger man. He rushed down the narrow aisle which stretched ribbonlike between rows of idle sewing machines. The effect was electric. Every worker jumped to her feet, and even the iciest inspector was magnetized by the encounter. At ground zero the eighty-one year old Meyer smashed Lasker in the face.

"Extortionist bastard, stealing my life's work," he sputtered, choking with anger.

"I don't see how you managed to stay open this long, old man," Lasker snarled, while using a silk handkerchief to wipe the trickle of blood seeping out of the corner of his nose.

"Nothing's changed," he yelled with rage. "It's you and these thugs you brought in here. You're crooks. Corrupt bastards, you and them," Ben continued, trembling uncontrollably. "You're trying to steal what you couldn't buy. My water's been turned off 'indefinitely for emergency repairs.' Tax audits. Asbestos. . ." Ben trailed off into his private nightmare.

"The City's running by the book for a change," Lenny opined contemptuously.

"This town would close down if it were run by the book," the son replied, more in disgust than anger.

Ben's eyes scoured in every direction for an impartial judge. He had been in America too long to accept what his employees instinctively knew from more recent experience with bureaucratic terrorism—he was done for.

"Max, will you talk to your old man or I'll take back my offer. I'm doing you people a favor and this is the gratitude I get," Lasker said, being used to unashamedly lying in people's faces.

"Stop it, Dad. It's not worth a heart attack." Max gently placed his arm around Ben's sagging shoulders.

"We've got two hundred people working here. What do they do? What do we do? This is our business." Ben's tone grew more despondent.

"Take a million dollars and go to Palm Beach," Lasker shot back with a satanic grin.

Max was stunned.

"One million? You offered us two million last month."

"Sell it to someone else," Lasker dared.

"What's left to sell," Ben whispered in a hobbled tone.

"Then it's a deal," Lasker pressed.

"Leave my father alone. We'll sign the papers."

Lasker snapped two fingers and his attorney stepped forward with a contract.

Ben was helped off the factory floor by his son, muttering "no conscience," while Max hung his head. The Meyers were familiar with adversity, but not with shame.

Lenny hurried from the factory. At the front door, he stopped in his tracks before a cardboard sign reading "DRESS OPERATORS WANTED." Lasker vindictively ripped and tossed the sign into the street.

As the limo slid from the curb, Lenny forgot the dingy loft he had just pillaged. His mind's eye already beheld new offices on the site, in competition with their richer older sisters across the East River. Lenny sank contentedly into the limo's soft maroon upholstery, flipped on an NFL replay without sound, and hit the cellular phone's recall button, which automatically dialed Anselmo's office number.

CHAPTER NINE

Anselmo's office was located in a converted catering hall. The front portion consisted of a sparsely furnished ballroom with scuffled spruce floors. Heavy wooden benches marked by three generations of initials, hearts, love poems, and other original carvings pressed up against whitewashed walls. One wall sported a huge banner alerting everyone that this was the Bayridge Democratic Club, Councilman Frank Anselmo District Leader. In very small letters at the bottom, as if the locals were dealing with something far away from home, it also announced FRANK ANSELMO, STATE DEMO-CRATIC CHAIRMAN. An American flag and a battered lectern stood beneath it. The center of the room was filled with stubby metal folding chairs, permanently kept open for club and community meetings, or for old folks to wile the hours away.

Everybody was welcome at the Baybridge Democratic Club, and municipal job applicants, politicians, community activists, senior citizens, handicapped, moguls, and felons all showed up at one time or another. There were no admission rules to this club, except one. On primary and election days, all hands had to be on deck to pull out the vote.

Anselmo operated from what was the catering establishment's kitchen. His office was a potpourri of memories. Shelves that once housed pots and pans still stood, filled instead with signposts that someone who mattered lived here. The Hibernian Society, Jewish Theological Seminary, Archdiocese, United Methodist Churches, Lighthouse for the Blind, Sons of Italy, March of Dimes, Friends of Maimonides Hospital, Children's Aid Society, Governor's Scholarship Committee, Columbia University, and literally hundreds of other equally prestigious awarders of medals, certificates, and statues testified that Anselmo was an important and generous man.

The kitchen's old brick oven was cold and dark now, except for one fresh, red rose which was placed daily in a thin glass vase at the mouth of this odd shrine to Anselmo's mother.

The office walls were totally covered with a museum-quality collection of autographed celebrity photographs of Anselmo with presidents, popes, rabbis, singers, comedians, movie stars, Nobel laureates, athletes, tycoons, and Mother Teresa. Anselmo's desk was barren of paper. Everything worth knowing was filed in his head. Pictures of his wife, children, and grandchildren covered the left corner of his desk. Alone on the right side stood a picture of a starry-eyed young Anselmo looking straight out into the future with John F. Kennedy.

Anselmo was busy signing pictures of himself with constituents for their regular monthly mailing. From time to time, he admiringly held one up to the fluorescent light above him and broke into a big smile on the heels of a pleasant memory. He put down his felt-tip pen and opened a side drawer in response to ringing on his private telephone.

"Hello," Anselmo answered inquiringly.

"I got it! I got everything! The factory. The land. Everything's right down to the waterline," gushed Lasker, still feasting on his victory over the Meyers. He resented their prolonged struggle, which had offended "Lasker's Law," that the weak should willingly serve the strong. And secretly, so closeted that the tycoon could not understand why he felt inferior to his victim, he was jealous of old man Meyer's commitment and courage.

"Lenny, I only did what was right. The place was a firetrap. It's only right for the city's inspectors to go after places that are not up to code," Anselmo replied matter-of-factly, brushing off Lasker's enthusiasm.

Anselmo didn't like Lasker much personally. These bourgeois billionaires were rootless. He never could tell which side they would fall on. But politics was a business and Lenny had contributed $350,000 to the party last year through seventy separate corporate entities. Anselmo recalled Lenny dumping a sack of checks on his bare desk, all legally proper corporate donations from such prosaic entities as 1410 Yellowstone Boulevard Corporation, Sedgewick Towers Corporation, Riverdale Terrace Inc., and so forth. Next year there would be both mayoral and City Council elections and the machine would need Lasker again.

"It was beautiful. One hundred percent legal," waxed Lasker.

"Money helps," Anselmo chuckled.

"Cheap, at any cost. Meyer's back was so far up against the wall, I knocked my own offer down a mil—"

Anselmo cut him off summarily. "You got what you wanted, why cheat and humiliate them? Pay the full price."

"Are you nuts?" Lasker said with the astonishment of having heard something of insane proportions.

"Never piss on the proud ones when they're down," Anselmo warned with the seriousness of one sharing a priceless principle. He remembered the most improbable encounters in which czars of New York were brought to ruin through short-sighted treatment of little guys who were friends or enemies. Anselmo was a facilitator. For him, less was more, if he achieved the desired end. Sociopaths like Lasker were dangerous.

"Now I must upgrade the assemblage from manufacturing zoning to commerical. And I need the City to build a subway station and highway off-ramp near BancExchange," Lenny said reminding Anselmo of their deal.

"Don't worry about it," Anselmo offered reassuringly.

"I'm serious. Without the zoning change, the place is dead. I've got a lot tied up in this assemblage," Lasker said in a voice filled with anxiety.

"Pop a cork. It's a lock. You can sleep on it," Anselmo replied with the contractual authority of a power broker who has given his word.

"And I wasn't kidding about paying Meyer the full price you promised. It's a deal breaker, Lenny. You don't pay Meyer two million dollars, no zoning, no infrastructure." Lasker knew Anselmo wasn't bluffing. The threat was crystal clear.

"Okay, don't get so excited. Just get the mayor aboard," Lenny agreed.

Anselmo turned back with great satisfaction to his community day clubhouse business. This was the kind of politics he loved. Old fashioned one-on-one, leader and constituent politics. Local folks in his district would come to Anselmo, once each week without any need for an appointment, and wait on the wooden folding chairs and benches outside his office for an audience. They could present their problems to Anselmo, much like to a priest or minister, except Anselmo could often do something tangible to solve them here on earth.

Government had become so distant and bureaucratically complex that it was indeed a disaster when an ordinary citizen had to rely on it. Anselmo was the navigator for the poor and middle class, much as the politically connected lawyers and lobbyists served rich businessmen. Anselmo's services were free. His rewards were ardent volunteers who stuffed envelopes, handed out leaflets, got nominating petitions signed, manned election-day phones and drove the vehicles to the polls during voter-pull operations. These were the loyal foot soldiers who served as infantry in Anselmo's powerful political machine.

Anselmo motioned to Clara to send in his next visitor. Clara sat at her metal desk outside of Anselmo's office much as she had done for the last thirty-three years, looking over the supplicants with the demeanor of a customs agent. She either gave reassurance to those who were just lonely or needed sympathy, or passed through anyone whom she believed "the Boss" could help.

Clara escorted an elderly woman into Anselmo's presence. Gussie needed no introduction and Anselmo hugged her. With a courtly bow he motioned Gussie to please be seated. As much as Anselmo had behaved as an iron-fisted Boss to Lenny, he presented himself as a friend and leader to a distraught Gussie, a gentleman whom she could count on to do things the old-fashioned way.

"They're gonna throw me out, Mr. Anselmo," she said knowing that this was her court of last resort.

"No one's gonna throw you out, Gussie," Anselmo replied with such assurance that her wrinkled face momentarily lit up with a smile; but it quickly turned back to a frown when she realized that nothing specific had been decided to get her out of jeopardy.

"He says I'm underoccupied. Can I help it if my daughter moves out? Isn't she entitled to a life of her own?" Hers was a simple plea for common-sense justice in a world run by regulations.

"Of course. How is Helene? Still working at the navy yard?" Frank was not shy about reminding constituents of past favors.

"Thanks to you. What can you do for me?" Gussie addressed Anselmo with the humility of his worshiper rather than the expectation of a demander.

"Just see that Mr. Brill obeys the law. You're grandfathered in over there. And if he tells you you're not, just give me a call. A curvy landlord like Morty Brill's always looking for a way around rent control. But how would he understand a law that was meant for working stiffs like you and me?"

Anselmo's name alone would probably intimidate Brill, because he could no longer count on Gussie being lost in the eternal maze of the City's rent-stabilization board. One phone call and an Anselmo bureaucratic dependent would issue a violation to Brill. The landlord would now choose to attack easier prey than Gussie.

Relief and joy danced in her eyes. She took Anselmo by the hand and issued an invitation.

"Oh thank you, Mr. Anselmo. You wanna come speak to my club?"

Clara moved close to Anselmo's desk and bent over to whisper in his ear. Anselmo glanced over Clara's shoulder to see Schwartz of the probation department waiting, nervously fingering his hat. Anselmo indicated to Clara "in a minute."

"What club is that, Gussie?"

"The Terrible Tiles Mahjong Club"

"How many Tiles belong?"

"A hundred and twelve," Gussie said proudly.

"You got it, sweetheart!" Anselmo's polite curiosity turned to avaricious interest, once he heard that a large number of likely voters would be his captive audience. "Just tell me when," he said slurping the mother's milk of politics.

Anselmo trotted pretentiously to meet Schwartz, feigning interest in an unpleasant task.

"Hello, Larry," he said enthusiastically.

"I have to see you, Frank." There was desperation in Schwartz's voice and perspiration on his forehead.

"Well, here I am. How about a cup of coffee?" Anselmo tried to make light of something neither of them took lightly.

"No thanks. We got to talk! You finished?" Schwartz was not going to give up his sense of urgency.

Anselmo surveyed his club for a moment; a few stragglers seeking favors; party workers licking envelopes; someone working a phone; paper plates and food scraps being cleaned up by elderly women.

"The business of government, Larry, is never finished," Anselmo said moving his hand in a sweeping motion which encompassed the people working or waiting in the clubhouse. "Let's take a walk," Anselmo communicated it as an order.

Anselmo and Schwartz descended the steep stairway in silence, which connected the converted catering hall to Fifth Avenue. They walked slowly among scores of morning shoppers, past busy mom-and-pop stores selling Genoa salami, fresh homemade pasta, provolone, Milanese baby outfits, oversized dresses, men's big and tall, work clothes, boots and shoes, Milanese magazines, and other necessities of life in this intact bastion of Italian neighborhood life. Down the street they entered Fino's, a diner crowded daily with local merchants who ate the early-bird special

lunch at 11 AM so they could serve their customers during the busy midday hours.

Mr. and Mrs. Fino each hugged Anselmo
with the lavish warmth which New York res-
tauranteurs reserved for "regulars." But then
again, Fino's only had "regulars," because
Bayridge, Brooklyn, like many small towns
that dot the American landscape, had few visitors and didn't miss them much. As with the
elites of Charleston, South Carolina, when
Bayridge folk spoke of one another, there was
always a contextual reference to the subject's
grandparents, parents, siblings, uncles or
cousins, and of course their children. Several
generations often lived together in the neat
two- and three-family homes which lined this
old neighborhood, and collateral relatives usually salted blocks in every direction.

Larry Schwartz's shoulders were hunched
in fear as he moved alongside an apparently
jovial Anselmo, who shook hands and exchanged jokes with friends sitting at the diner's counter and around its Formica-topped
tables. Not one person in Fino's would have
acknowledged seeing Larry Schwartz with Anselmo. In this tightly woven community, people minded their own business, especially
when a local hero, such as Frank Anselmo was
involved. After what seemed like an eternity
for a perspiring Schwartz, they finally settled

into a corner booth that always remained free for Anselmo's exclusive use.

A waiter accented by his well-worn chianti-red apron, about Anselmo's age, instantaneously set down glasses of water and cups of coffee with a lively greeting: "Mr. A?"

"Fine. How are you?"

On cue the waiter burst out in song:

"I'm as corny as Kansas in August.
I'm as normal as blueberry pie.
No more a smart little girl with no heart.
I have found me a wonderful guy."

Anselmo first conducted the tune and then joined in singing its last line. The crooners dissolved into laughter, while Schwartz's mouth fell open. The lost little boy in Schwartz wanted to cry in anguish over his disappearing life. Could it be that his fate rested in the hands of a madman?

Anselmo was royalty at Fino's, and he naturally maintained the dignity and lightness expected of him by his subjects. Ignoring the barely subdued internal screams of his guest, Anselmo turned to the server. "Speaking of blueberry pies, buy us a couple." And looking at Schwartz, he asked, "À la mode?"

"I don't want any pie," Schwartz replied with the sullenness of a neglected child.

"Two blueberry pies à la mode," Anselmo responded without missing a beat.

As the server sashayed away chuckling amidst humming the bridge to "A Wonderful Guy," Anselmo's smile became a very businesslike grimace.

"What's the matter, Larry?" he disingenuously inquired.

"You know what's the matter," a pouting Schwartz responded.

"You look terrible, you ought to take a vacation," Anselmo said trying to get Schwartz to lighten up.

Instead, Schwartz enumerated a litany of things which he had at stake:

"I don't want a vacation. I got eighteen years in, I've saved up my time. I'm eligible for pension in six months if I put in the hours . . ."

Schwartz had turned bitter in the face of Frank's seeming indifference, so Anselmo interrupted with a show of concern. "Okay, why, what is it?"

"Get the deputy mayor off my ass," Schwartz hurled at him, with as much implicit threat as request.

"Couldn't you handle him?"

"It was easy. Too easy," Schwartz responded in a whispered reflection. Larry carried enough scar tissue from bureaucratic wars to intuitively know that Kevin Calhoun was dangerously different.

Fino's featured non-stop show-tune music in the background. When Frank entered, Mr. Fino, as always, had popped a Rodgers and Hammerstein medley into the stereo. The server now quickly swept out, in time with the music from behind the counter, balancing pies with ice cream. He set them on the table with a deep bow and was startled when Schwartz pushed his plate away from in front of him; Larry just stared into the middle distance, frustrated. Anselmo and the waiter deliberately ignored this intrusion into their ritual. Frank exited his booth with a stylized bow and in a beautiful baritone sang a solo:

> "Don't throw bouquets at me.
> Don't please my folks too much.
> Don't laugh at my jokes too much . . ."

And locking arms with the waiter, they joined in a duet finale:

"People will say we're in love!"

As the waiter scurried away laughing to wait on another table, Schwartz's despair provoked an angry defiance.

"What the hell was that?" His tone implied

"why are you clowning around, while my life ebbs away?"

"He and I are great Rodgers and Hammerstein fans. 'When you walk through a storm, keep your head up high,' Larry," Frank said advisedly.

Anselmo knew from experience that when you have a mess on your hands, no action is better than taking action which can't influence the outcome and might actually hurt it. If you ride it out, dangers usually go away.

"It's not your signature on that probation report," Schwartz shot back.

Frank caught the threat and in the sharp tone of Boss he warned, "And watch your mouth."

Anselmo finished his pie slowly to underline that he would not be blackmailed. Unspecified negative consequences for disobedience were clearly the subcontext when, after taking his last bite of pie, Anselmo told Schwartz coldly, "And take a vacation."

He then reached across the table and took a big forkful of Schwartz's blueberry pie and swallowed it down, while Larry stared at Anselmo in nervous despair.

CHAPTER TEN

Mayor Pappas understood that powerful men loved to be heralded when they arrived in New York, because it made them feel less anonymous in the world's busiest and most powerful city. He therefore sent New York's equivalent of Roman chariots and trumpets, an elite police motorcycle unit with full siren, to escort Senator and Mrs. Marquand from LaGuardia Airport to a small dinner party in their honor at Gracie Mansion.

Senator Marquand had a rush of self-importance when he gazed through the front windshield at two helmeted motorcycle cops shepherding the motorcade along the white median divider line, amidst wall-to-wall traffic on the Long Island Expressway. Outriders on each side forced reluctant drivers to move into other lanes at odd angles, and two cyclists at the rear kept cars from tailing too closely behind the limousine. The senator had that satisfied grin of a little boy who had received the toy he always dreamed of when he told his wife in a soft cultivated southern drawl, "That John Pappas sure knows how to welcome a man."

Mrs. Marquand's acquiescing smile buttressed her husband's pride at having truly arrived.

The motorcade streaked past the city-operated basketball courts at the Ninety-sixth Street exit of the Franklin Delano Roosevelt Drive, filled with youthful ghetto wannabe-champs playing their hearts out under bright night lights. The motorcade crossed Manhattan's demilitarized zone, which defined more than geography in the designation north or south of Ninety-sixth Street, and turned left onto East End Avenue, lined with towering luxury apartment houses. The lead escorts guided the motorcade into an abrupt broken U-turn across East End Avenue. Suddenly, leaving the intense city behind, they rode briefly up what could have been a country road winding through trees, hedges, and lawns to arrive at Gracie Mansion.

Gracie Mansion felt at home in the bucolic surroundings of Carl Schurz Park since Archibald Gracie, a Scottish-born merchant, built it in 1799 as a majestic farmhouse on a low hill flowing down to a wide bend in the East River. In 1887 the City seized it for non-payment of taxes from the Gracie family, and in 1942 Mayor Fiorello LaGuardia, "The Little Flower," designated it as the official mayoral residence.

Senator and Mrs. Marquand stepped off the cobblestone path and onto a broad wooden front porch. An incredible East River vista rolled out in front of them. On this clear chilly evening, they couldn't help but feel the sharp comparison of the elegant simplicity and protection offered by Gracie Mansion's early Federal style and commanding acreage to the seething complexity of Queens in the foreground across the river.

The mayor and his wife poured through their front door, wearing no coats on this wintry night, and intercepted the Marquands with generous handshakes and hugs on the porch. Their spontaneous greetings and warm words ended the diplomatic inhibitions strangers normally encounter in such official situations. The Washington emissary would now be able to enjoy the mayor's genuine social hospitality while discussing his disposition to bring the

Democratic National Convention to New York City.

Downtown from the festivities at Gracie Mansion, Judge Stern waited until the darkness of a winter night, before he dared leave his courthouse. Bone was finally left standing alone, except for a Japanese television crew which filmed him as part of a documentary on violence in America. Stern's self-assured stride had turned into a slow bowed walk. As the judge descended the broad courthouse steps, he involuntarily found himself moving closer to Bone, until he could plainly stare at the victim's destroyed visage. Then with tortured glances from side to side, he stole spastically down the naked stone steps into the blackness, a modern day Cain afraid to look over his shoulder.

Power was always the main course at a Gracie Mansion dinner party. And tonight Senator Marquand was its axis. He had the goods which Mayor Pappas wanted delivered: the selection of New York City as the Democratic National Convention site and the coronation of Pappas as its keynote speaker.

Protocol Chief Warner Chapin had studied

every detail of Marquand's background before fashioning the invitations. The guest list combined the concept of catering to the senator's known interests and tastes with the New York reality that you are what you do: Richard Jenrette, CEO of Equitable Life Assurance Company was a native son of the senator's state of South Carolina, with family still thriving at the center of Charleston society; Greenwich Village's Frank Stella, a founding father of the contemporary movememt, played to Marquand's new-found interest in modern art; Professor Allen Brinkley had been consulted by Marquand, based on his insightful work on the history of the American presidency; Rand Araskog, chairman of the powerful ITT Corporation, was owner of the Madison Square Garden Convention site; and Torsten Wiesel, Nobel Prize-winning President of Rockefeller University, had recently received praise for his defense of basic scientific research before Senator Marquand's committee.

The protocol chief could reasonably expect that this eclectic group and their spouses would probably know one another, or at least of each other, from New York's A+ dinner party circuit and interdisciplinary professional activities. These sophisticated guests would also be able to speak on, and more importantly listen to, any topic which the senator might wish to engage.

While typical dinner parties have guests principally speaking to their neighbors on the right and left, at Gracie Mansion there is generally a unified conversation center around the mayor and his principal guest. Senator Marquand sat ramrod straight, somewhat intimidating those with lesser posture, as he watched his favorite dish, Charleston shrimp pilau, being served by the Gracie Mansion chef. Simultaneously, the senator held court at the table.

". . . I'll never forget that afternoon last month in the committee room. TV cameras rolling, the gallery filled, what a risk you took . . ."

The mayor gently waved his hand and said, "No risk, the guy was wrong."

With four-term senators like Marquand, however, "right and wrong" was played out over the long run, not issue by issue. Therefore, proper process and protocol were as important as substance.

"But no mayor, I don't care if he is from New York, tells off a cabinet member like that. Secretary of urban development, that's the hand that feeds the cities . . ."

"Not very well," Mayor Pappas replied playfully.

"Well, he's your enemy for life," Marquand responded earnestly, reemphasizing the importance of relationships in politics.

There was a subcontext to the conversation between the senator and mayor. Marquand understood Pappas was seeking to carve out an identity for a presidential run someday, but he felt that it was premature to be confrontational. Marquand was the type of Senate insider who was too busy running the country to run for the presidency himself. But he was a kingmaker, who felt he knew the route best. The cardinal rule was to make as few enemies as possible along the way.

"A man's stature is not made by the friends he makes, but by his enemies," Pappas said, bluntly refocusing on his need to establish an independent identity.

"It also got you the cover of *Time*," said Mrs. Marquand, relieving her husband's admonition with a little recognition that Pappas was indeed succeeding in getting attention.

"You've definitely gone national, Mayor Pappas. They're even beginning to take you seriously at the Business Round Table," Araskog added, referring to the nation's leading group of big business CEOs.

"And that 'stature' thing. Who said that?" Mrs. Marquand said teasingly to Mayor Pappas, as if to now bring him down to size.

"I did, just now. I had an acute attack of self-importance but here's just the guy to cut me down to size. Kevin, we missed you!" Mayor Pappas's face lit up with the entrance of his deputy.

"Sorry, folks, didn't mean to interrupt," Kevin mumbled as he tried to unobtrusively take a seat while the servant had discreetly added next to Mayor Pappas.

"Kevin's been busy today, I'll bet," Senator Marquand said with affection, seeking to re-establish their personal relationship from days past in Washington.

"Hello, Senator," Kevin said both respect-fully and warmly.

Calhoun knew most of the guests and was introduced by the mayor to the others.

Jenrette interrupted the Mayor's introduc-tion. "I know Kevin; we were on the phone today on the BancExchange thing. I don't know how he made time for me considering what happened."

"Indeed, we don't want any stray bullets around Madison Square Garden," Senator Marquand said puckishly. He was signaling Pappas that this kind of publicity hurts the city's chances at a critical time, and that it should be cleaned up as quickly and quietly as possible.

"Ignore him, Kevin, the senator just likes to

keep a little anchor to windward," the mayor responded with a faux school master's tone, while alerting Marquand that he got the message.

"Don't we all? But in the meantime, shouldn't we return to the burning issue of the day, the convention?" said Mrs. Pappas, trying to bring back the positive tone of the conversation and to help get some commitment for the convention. Senator Marquand took note of her smooth segue, and recorded in his mind that Mrs. Pappas would be a political asset to her husband in a future national race.

Before anyone could respond, Calhoun jumped in, and addressed Senator Marquand. "Senator, we're going to turn this city upside down for you. We're going to stage the right kind of convention . . ."

"What kind is that?" Marquand asked.

"The kind that's going to get the president re-elected. Where are you going to go, second cities like Chicago? Always resonates with memories of riots in 'sixty-eight. California? Where you still smell char from the South Central fires. Miami? Miami's Casablanca. We'll make you a winner, we've got the world-class city right here."

An awkward moment of silence was broken by Mrs. Marquand, who echoed everyone's sentiment at listening to Kevin's passionate pitch.

"Hey, I love this guy."

"The line forms to the left. And don't try to steal him from us," Mayor Pappas said proudly putting his arm across Kevin's shoulders.

And to affirm his reaction to the dinner, Marquand added the critical lines: "Give me a call in the morning, Kevin, I need some stuff in *The New York Times*; an editorial lauding our potential choice of New York as Convention City. The president loves a good *Times* editorial."

"You got it, and let me say, Senator . . ."

Calhoun was so wound up, he continued selling the convention proposition, even though the senator had stood up to leave, so the mayor interrupted his over-enthusiastic Deputy with a broad grin and said, "The vote's in, Kevin. We'll get the convention. Now let these people go, they're running for the last shuttle."

"We miss you on the Hill, m'friend. The staffers still talk about the wunderkind on Ways and Means." Marquand smiled and patted Kevin lavishly on the back. He turned to the mayor and suggested only half-jokingly, "This guy had the means to the end. But don't forget, John, we taught him everything he knows."

The mayoral hosts exchanged warm good-byes with their departing guests and took a few steps into the smaller, less formal sitting room on the left side of Gracie Mansion's large entrace foyer. The mayor, Mrs. Pappas, and Kevin simultaneously plopped into the deeply piled couches with fully outstretched legs, as if in rebellious reaction to the implicit pressure throughout dinner of mimicking Senator Marquand's perfect posture. Noticing their uniform spontaneous responses, all three started laughing uproariously.

Then turning to Kevin, Mrs. Pappas piped up with a motherly smile: "You want something to eat, Kevin?"

"Nothing, thanks," he replied in the voice of someone who didn't want to cause a fuss, even though he was really starving.

"Kevin's been so busy devouring his work, I bet he hasn't eaten anything digestible all day," Mayor Pappas said with awareness of Kevin's intonation. "Honey, tell the kitchen to fix him a hamburger and onions on a toasted bun."

Mrs. Pappas threw a cherishing look at both men, in appreciation of the tender affection and respect which united them in a father-son relationship; she felt that the mayor needed a young male protégé to help fill the hole left by their only son's death in Vietnam. As she exited toward the kitchen, the mayor uttered his usual, "What's new, Kevin?"

"Tino Zapatti's bullet killed the child, not the cop's." Silence reigned. "That's it," said Kevin.

"Is that what passes for good news these days?" The mayor's expression exhibited the expectation that the first misfortune in the Bone case was just the opening scene in a miserable full-length play.

"Well, I'll take it," said Kevin, shifting his thoughts to reporting his preliminary conclusions to the boss. "I saw Tino's probation report," Kevin continued. "Exemplary, but an odd thing . . ."

"What?"

"It's front-loaded."

"With what?"

"Supervisory personnel," Kevin said, thinking about the thousand times he tried unsuccessfully to get supervisors to participate in the City's daily working matters.

"Got signed off on by an honest judge," the mayor observed.

"Yes, Walter Stern," muttered Calhoun, much like a detective determinedly roaming the crime scene, picking up bits and pieces of the puzzle.

"Thank God," the mayor offered with a simplicity that covered years of training in the more cynical world of politics. The mayor sighed with the uncertain relief, more of a prayer, that people would let go when they realized that the parole was just an honest mistake.

Kevin next briefed the mayor on Lasker's high-pressured acquisition of the Meyers' factory space, emphasizing that the additonal land was not integral to a successful BancExchange project, but merely a vehicle for the landlord to reap more profit. Calhoun saw Anselmo's fine hand behind the City agencies' selective crackdown at Meyer & Son, thereby forcing the sale to Lasker. He raised the question as to whether the City should tolerate such needless gentrification, at the expense of the poor, or if it should use its zoning powers and needed infrastructure expenditures near the site to force Lasker to forego the Meyers' property. And in any case, he added, the current City budget couldn't afford another new subway station and highway off-ramp.

"I'm meeting Frank Anselmo for breakfast. I'm trying to work things out," Kevin said energetically.

"Where?"

"Woerner's."

"The pols' hangout near Brooklyn Borough Hall?"

"That's it."

Mayor Pappas detected his deputy's eagerness for the confrontation with Anselmo, which he wanted to dampen.

"When you go to Brooklyn, you're Frank Anselmo's guest. Don't piss up his leg. Just get him off the infrastructure thing. Nothing wrong with it, no link to Meyers or anything else, but unaffordable now. Take Anselmo to the edge, but not over it. And good work tonight."

"You think it went okay? Mrs. Marquand couldn't stop talking about the cover of *Time*," Kevin said cheerfully.

"I think she collects them," the mayor threw off with a guileless smile.

"National ink. It's the mother's milk of politics," Calhoun yelled ebulliently. "What do you think, boss, is the vote in? Did I hear us get the convention?"

"It's not signed and sealed yet, but I think it is delivered. You were the closer," the mayor said admiringly of his deputy.

"I thought I had him with the Second City sutff," the youthful Kevin waxed ever more enthusiastically.

"Of course you did. You know why? It belongs here! New York! This is the place."

Mayor Pappas spoke with the same true believer's passion, that had attracted Kevin to his ranks. But when the mayor caught his own act, he sheepishly laughed at himself.

Jamie the Intel man appeared and pointed to his watch in response to the mayor's earlier request for a reminder when the eleven o'clock news would go on.

"The Bone story is being featured on Eyewitness News," Kevin indicated with a click of the TV remote. And there it was, the lead story on Channel 7, click; the lead story on Channel 2; click, the lead story on Channel 4.

"Enough," Pappas said sharply.

"They're all over it like a cheap suit," Calhoun observed with helpless disdain.

"And it's going to stick to us like one," the mayor sighed in grim resignation.

Each night at 11:30 PM, an Intel bodyguard delivered the first edition of the *Daily News*, the *New York Post* and *The New York Times* to the mayor. Public officials were probably the only persons, among the tiny number of people who actually read newspaper editorials at all, who studied editorial columns with the precision normally accorded to religious scrolls.

"Get this in the *Times* editorial: 'Judge Or Be Judged,'" Kevin remarked showing some agitation.

" '. . . the last identifiable vestige of graft.' What the hell are they talking about? Judges get nominated and elected like anybody else," the mayor shouted.

"The *appearance* of process. You know the party de facto controls who becomes a Judge," Kevin responded without leaving much room for doubt.

The mayor rejoined his deputy, with the reality that the democratic dream had become a nightmare of the public's own making: "It needn't be that way, if the newspapers would cover the damn local elections and people cared enough to vote in them. It's easy to complain. But citizens have to assume some responsibility for their own democracy, or expect that others will take it from them. A power vacuum is always filled by the few who care enough, whatever their purposes. Voters and their newspapers should grow up and do their duty, or stop whining," Mayor Pappas said slamming the *Times* on the lamp table beside him.

"But do we have to be part of the civic decline," Calhoun asked cautiously.

"Whose side are you on?"

"Yours, John. And I always will be. I sense a hanging party. Maybe we should put a little distance between us and Walter Stern—"

Kevin suggested before he was abruptly cut off by the Mayor.

"Distance is shit. Distance is what you do to your enemies. It's an invention of the nineties to make friends extinct." The mayor leveled his eyes on his deputy mayor with a resolve that reflected his deepest convictions. "You're good, but still young. You don't run from friends in trouble because it's convenient for you. You're a man first, a politician second. We're sticking by Judge Walter Stern."

"I hear you," was the only response Calhoun could think of.

CHAPTER ELEVEN

Although Fino's and Woerner's were both Anselmo's hangouts in Brooklyn, these restaurants could well have catered to people from different planets. While Fino's was home to Bayridge's blue-collar families for generations, Woerner's was populated by every transient species in New York's political food chain: small time Court Street lawyers, lobbyists, fixers, district leaders, Supreme Court judges, bail bondsmen, city marshals, state legislators, councilmen, and every form of political hanger-on. Since all of these denizens of Woerner's had offices nearby in the Borough Hall vicinity, runners kept appearing and withdrawing with envelopes containing official-looking documents. Politics was the only topic of conversation at Woerner's, particularly the who's in—who's out variety of gossip, rather than any issue-oriented discussions. And prosperity seemed to be weighed by the pound, since more huge men could be seen at Woerner's tables than anywhere else in Brooklyn.

There was nothing permanent about the clientele at Woerner's. They were eating breakfast there by grace of their position, measured and remeasured day to day by everyone in the restaurant, in the City's bureaucratic and political power structure. If one lost an election, got indicted, found himself fired or, God forbid, succumbed to a human frailty such as chronic illness, he would instantly become an invisible man among his "friends" at Woerner's. And both victims and predators accepted such ostracism as part of the natural order in Woerner's political jungle.

In a tight, nearly partitioned-off area, Anselmo was surrounded by Murray Safire, an amiable lobbyist-fixer, Lenny Lasker, the real estate glutton, and three non-descript commissioners who unquestioningly did their boss' bidding in the bowels of New York City's bureaucracy. The group was schmoozing while impatiently waiting for Deputy Mayor Calhoun to arrive. Lenny puffed incessantly on his cigarette; the others periodically reached through his veil of smoke to break off a piece of Danish from a platter regularly refilled by a zealous old waiter.

Anselmo gestured for Calhoun to come over quickly when he spotted him at the door. The group at the table noisily scraped their chairs as they slid over to create a space for Calhoun opposite Anselmo.

"You get lost?" Anselmo asked gruffly, in the face of Calhoun's apparent show of disrespect.

"Somewhere there's a key to downtown Brooklyn, but I sure don't have it," Calhoun said quietly in apology.

"Sit, sit, sit down already; take a load off your feet," Safire ordered Calhoun in casual greeting.

As Calhoun joined the table, Anselmo gently admonished him for having pretense. "And why don't you get yourself a driver, for Chrissake? After three years, the 'clean as a hound's tooth' image is beginning to wear."

As the group chuckled at Calhoun's initiation to Woerner's humor, as if by signal the ancient waiter set down plates of fried eggs and bacon and hashbrowns. The waiter stood by for Calhoun's order.

"What'll you have?" Anselmo prodded him.

"Oatmeal with skim milk and sliced bananas, please," ordered Calhoun.

A deathly silence fell over the table as the waiter shifted uncomfortably in his place, reacting as if he were the butt of a joke.

"What happened?" Calhoun asked in genuine bewilderment.

"Lenny just threw up," quipped Anselmo. And everyone burst into laughter as Anselmo ordered a "man's" breakfast for Calhoun: "Bring him ham and eggs—and because he's the mayor's boy, we'll indulge him, dry white toast instead of a bagel with cream cheese."

Calhoun smiled in knowing amusement at his own foibles and as acknowledgement that he didn't feel ill at ease being subjected to their good-natured ridicule.

"So what's new, Kevin?" was Anselmo's icebreaker.

Calhoun listed at least ten municipal thickets before his eye caught the tabloid headline exposed on the table, "Carver Crossfire Won't Go Away." Anselmo picked up on Calhoun's eye contact and interrupted his discourse with: "*Plus* a kid got shot."

"*And* a drug dealer," added Safire.

"*And* a cop," rejoined Anselmo.

"No wonder the deputy mayor joined us in Brooklyn today," Safire said mockingly.

"But he's very welcome," Anselmo replied turning to Calhoun.

"All that bad news. That's why we need

something positive for the city, like BancEx-change," injected Lenny, as he brought the discussion down to the business at hand.

"No argument, Lenny," Calhoun responded rapidly.

"So we need the full zoning envelope to upgrade from manufacturing to commercial, a subway stop and an off-ramp from the Brooklyn-Queens Expressway. Kevin, you on board for this afternoon's Council meeting?" asked Anselmo.

"As for infrastructure—" Kevin was cut-off by Anselmo, who said:

"Infrastructure is just a fancy word for the necessities of life."

"The city is twenty-five billion dollars in debt, Frank, we're in no position to build sub-way stops and off-ramps," Calhoun responded firmly.

"Three thousand workers and you don't want to build them a subway stop?" Lenny asked incredulously. "Infrastructure will help develop the rest of that run-down area into a taxable corporate gold coast for New York."

"Oh, did you also happen to buy a few op-tions on the property around BancExchange, Lenny? It's never enough, is it Lenny?" Cal-houn said sharply.

"Of course Lenny bought options. And so did every other developer in town, as soon as the deal was known. Notwithstanding who makes money, Mr. Deputy Mayor, it's great for the city. But if you don't have a way to transport their employees, BancExchange's going to dump this deal and move their back office *and* headquarters to New Jersey." Anselmo was overcome with anger at Calhoun's arrogant insistence that doing good for the city precluded individuals from doing well for themselves. The idea itself challenged the very premise of his political machine's existence.

"So be it. The mayor loves BancExchange, Frank, but he can't afford infrastructure." Calhoun stubbornly dug in his heels.

"The train's leaving the station, Kevin, don't you want to be aboard?" Anselmo asked his young adversary.

"You think you got the noses?" Calhoun inquired challengingly, with reference to that afternoon's forthcoming City Council vote on BancExchange.

"We haven't counted yet," Anselmo replied. And raising his eyebrows cynically, he said, "Why? I thought you were on our side. You're sure flying in the face of real politics. Infrastructure means jobs. And jobs means votes. I thought John Pappas liked votes. I know next year that he'll need votes." Anselmo wielded the twin currencies of politics masterfully, but

Kevin was too far down the track to put on the brakes:

"He loves votes, Frank. But no infrastructure. Much as the City approves of the idea of a subway station and off-ramp, it can't pay for them. And we haven't even begun to talk about why you want upzoning on 500,000 square feet of space beyond the needs of BancExchange."

Calhoun looked up to see Anselmo putting his coat on and walking toward the door with this entourage in tow. "Hey, where're you going?"

"I got an appointment in Manhattan," Anselmo responded matter-of-factly.

"The meeting's finished?" Kevin asked with genuine surprise.

"I heard you say 'no'," Anselmo replied decisively.

Calhoun paused a moment, remembering Mayor Pappas' urging him not to drive Anselmo over the edge. "Can I offer you a ride?" Kevin suggested in the hope of continuing negotiations.

"No thanks, I can make it quicker on the train," Anselmo said dismissively. And calling the deputy mayor's bet, the Boss set the stage for a high stages showdown at that afternoon's Council meeting.

CHAPTER TWELVE

Calhoun was mounting the broad marble steps of the circular staircase in City Hall's rotunda two at a time, aggressively on his way to the BancExchange shootout with Anselmo in the City Council legislative chambers, when he was practically run down by a young woman moving at an even faster pace. As she lapped Kevin on the steps and turned to look down at him eye-to-eye, he recognized her as the DEA lawyer who had spoken with the mayor and Mrs. Santos in the Kings County Hospital corridor.

Confronted with this human roadblock, Calhoun was forced to read the information on her business card, which had been thrust into his hand, "Detective Endowment Association, Legal Affairs, Co-counsel," as she made a breathless introduction: "Mr. Deputy Mayor, I'm Marybeth Cogan."

Absorbing the gestalt of a pretty woman with a minor functionary's title blocking his path to a vital City Council meeting, Calhoun simply blew Marybeth off with a "very nice" and tried to move around her. Cogan determinedly resumed her blocking position and said with indignation, "I represent Detective Eddie Santos and you're muddying my client's name."

Keeping on the move, both of them, Calhoun replied dismissively, "Why don't you take the matter up with Corporation Counsel?"

"And get it buried? No thank you. I've already tried every channel right up to the commissioner and had every door slammed in my face. Aren't you supposed to be the pipeline to the mayor? Tell him somebody's taking him up the wrong street," she shot back, punching the air with frustration.

Not failing to notice Marybeth's gentle beauty and lively eyes, and unable to avoid serving as the anvil for her sledgehammer commitment, he momentarily slowed his hasty footsteps and said, "Interesting. Could we explore this in more detail? Maybe over coffee or something."

"I'm talking about a hero detective and his widow's pension," she hurled back at him, choosing to ignore his sexist remark.

"And I'm heading for a Council meeting about a six hundred million dollar, three thousand job creating economic development project. So please excuse me . . . no, why don't you wait in my office."

"I don't think so, you've got my card. I'll expect to hear from you in the morning," she said rushing by him down the steps. The sheer energy of her purpose magnetically drew his eyes toward following her movement all the way through the front doors of City Hall.

Calhoun had not heard any new negative reports on Santos, since the speculation that swirled about on the day of the shooting. He shrugged his shoulders and proceeded hurriedly toward the City Council chamber.

As Calhoun passed into the Council chamber through tall leather-covered padded doors, he was maneuvered into a corner by Captain Florian of the Police Internal Affairs Unit.

In the background Kevin could hear the mechanical drone of Councilman Garrity proposing an Irish Hero Day of Celebration resolution, primarily for the record with his Irish nationalist constituents, which no one bothered to listen to, while in the foreground small clusters of councilmen huddled with Anselmo,

Lasker, and their minions in preparation for the BancExchange vote. Calhoun was relieved to see Abe and his soldiers from the mayor's government affairs division lobbying with equal intensity.

"I think we're going to have a problem in the Bone shooting. The dead cop might have been dirty," Florian whispered with the tone of a heads-up for the mayor.

"Where did you hear it?" Calhoun asked with sudden alertness to the issue.

"Internal Affairs is coming up with more and more signs of it. I think we better get out in front of this. It's always better politically, for the sake of the department, that we announce our bad apples ourselves," Florian offered with the assurance of a pro.

With a broken engine whine, the clerk introduced a routine zoning amendment: ". . . in the Borough of Queens, block seven-eight-four scheduled to rezone from residential R-1 to R-12 multiple dwelling. In the Borough of Queens, block six-four-four, from industrial R-12 to residential R-12 multiple dwelling . . ." The clerk's statement did not alter the indifference of the chamber, where everyone continued with his own business or conversations.

"I don't want police corruption headlines on the day of a cop's funeral; he has a family for Chrissakes," Calhoun spilled out.

"Maybe we can wait, but it's best to announce these things quickly. They always leak out," Florian countered.

"Do you have enough evidence?"

"It's getting there. By tomorrow I think we'll have it nailed down. So send the mayor out of town; he doesn't want to give a hero's eulogy to a cop who is going to be labeled dirty the next day," Florian murmured behind a palm wrapped around his mouth, so nobody could read his lips.

Florian melted back into the crowd, leaving Calhoun to wonder what was going on. Somebody was clearly putting out the word that Santos was dirty even before the hard evidence was in. But why? Who? Calhoun didn't have time for further reflection, because the public advocate rapped his wooden gavel twice to announce the final debate and vote on the BancExchange bill.

The sedate two-story City Council chamber, with its mahogany-and-white paneled Georgian-design walls, gold-leaf trim, and original oils depicting idealized portraits of the nation's founding fathers could give the impression, when empty, that it housed an orderly, deliberative democratic legislative process. But as Calhoun made his way down its central aisle to occupy a reserved folding chair next to one of several standing microphones, he passed through democracy's chaotic reality. Councilmen and spectators alike ignored the public advocate's rapping gavel, continuing to conduct their arguments, negotiations, conversations, and protests.

The City's top legislative officials and support staff filled in behind a raised mahogany judicial dais that stretched fifty feet in length across the front of the Council chamber. At its center, the public advocate occupied a red throne chair elevated above all of the others, although his offical role was more ceremonial than tangible.

All of the dais occupants peered down at the entire chamber, since it rested on a raised platform. Front and center below were fifty-one elected councilmen, seated at nineteenth century slanted writing desks. Since New York's neighborhoods were ethnically, racially, religiously, economically, and even sexually balkanized for the large part, constitutionally mandated local election districts produced a veritable visual and political mosaic of representatives. Consensus through ideological accommodation was extraordinarily difficult to achieve under these circumstances, an obstacle that the more homogenous democratic founding fathers didn't have to face.

Bills were enacted either because they were

so innocuous as to offend nobody, such as an unopposed street name change, or because the crisis was so bad that the alternative was collapse, such as with the fiscal crisis of 1977. All other legislation was enacted because a few powerful leaders forced a consensus. For example, the Council Speaker had absolute power to assign committees and chairmanships which paid $20,000 on top of the Councilman's paltry $50,000 base salary. Office perks, staff, and access to information were also weapons of his control. Electoral power brokers such as Anselmo were also decisive in imposing consensus, since they controlled important sources of local campaign financing and deliverable votes in the districts.

Off to the front left side of the dais were rows of metal folding chairs, filled with the print media, while five TV cameras and crews stood along that side of the chamber. Privileged staffers, lobbyists, and petitioners occupied every inch of space along the side walls for the important BancExchange vote.

In the back and in the balcony, ordinary citizens were packed behind roped cordons surrounded by burly, efficient sergeants-at-arms. Old Man Meyer and his son Ben stood out among the largely minority protesters in the balcony, who waved banners proclaiming "WORK NOT WELFARE" and "STOP GENTRIFYING

BLUE COLLAR WORKERS TO DEATH." On the opposite side of the balcony were familiar clubhouse faces marshaled by Anselmo; they wielded signs in the affirmative, such as "MIDDLE-CLASS JOBS—NEW YORK'S ENDANGERED SPECIES."

After incessant gavel-rapping and expert herding by the sergeants-at-arms, the City Council chamber came to momentary order. Theatrically, the public advocate cried, "The seven-hundred thirteenth meeting of the City council of the City of New York is now in session." And he turned to Councilman Anselmo to report to BancExchange bill out of the Land Use Committee which he chaired. "The Land Use Committee recommends passage of the BancExchange bill, which will create three thousand vitally needed middle class jobs. To make this possible, we recommend upzoning two million square feet of space from manufacturing to commercial office status. And that the City construct a thirty million dollar subway station and fifteen million dollar off-ramp to facilitate movement of people to and from the area."

"Something's happening," Calhoun leaned over and whispered to Abe beside him.

"I'm getting a serious infrastructure feeling," replied Abe shaking his head.

"Welcome aboard, Abe. Anselmo must have

picked up some votes for his bill. Grab Seymour. Tell him the mayor's office wishes to express some points of order concerning the legality of this legislation. Lasso him, if you have to, but get it done now."

Abe was seen whispering feverishly in the public advocate's ear. The advocate then rapped his gavel twice and said, "We will take a ten-minute recess from the legislative debate, during which Deputy Mayor Calhoun will address the assembled group on BancExchange." Anselmo whispered in the public advocate's other ear and with two more gavel raps the advocate announced, "Mr. Lenny Lasker, developer of the BancExchange project, will also be invited to provide information during this informal proceeding."

The deputy mayor stood before the microphone in the central aisle, and for the first time there was absolute silence in the chamber.

"Mr. Public Advocate, the mayor's office objects to rezoning on block eight-four-seven. We're asking a delay for further study." The folks in the balcony stirred perceptibly as they leaned forward on the edges of their chairs.

Lasker's eyes caught Anselmo's in frozen shock. And the public advocate, holding up his agenda, said, "Mr. Deputy Mayor, but that item has already been approved by the planning commission."

"There are several hundred blue collar jobs in jeopardy in a portion added subsequently to the application's approval. Approval was granted for 1.5 million square feet, not two million. The City Charter mandates economic development hearings and reconsideration in such cases," Calhoun continued in a manner which increasingly showed him to be a commanding presence.

Leonard Lasker rose before the other microphone on the opposite side of the central aisle.

"Mr. President, this site is an environmental hazard. We are lucky there haven't been any deaths at that location. This is a delaying tactic on the part of the former owners who once again wish to victimize their employees. And delay would occur, while my interest clock is still ticking!"

"That may be, but the City Charter mandates we cannot bulldoze working men and women onto the welfare rolls just to make room for some fancy office space that is not clearly integrated with the originally approved BancExchange project, without an economic development hearing. It's the law," shouted Calhoun in decisive defiance.

"Mr. President, please! This is ridiculous! We need jobs. The city is desperate. Where do we expect to employ the people who pay taxes in this city?" Lasker pleaded with a flushed face.

"There are laws that govern zoning changes and job loss," Calhoun repeated stubbornly.

"Mr. President, this is idiotic. We've already put aside a five thousand dollar relocation fee for every employee displaced at Meyer & Son," Lasker offered, extending his palms in a gesture of generosity, while his lawyer pulled frantically at his sleeve to shut up.

A chorus of boos echoed forth from the workers in the balcony.

"I submit that Mr. Lasker's own admission requires a delay," Calhoun said, pointing to the zoning resolution. "There is no record of a relocation fee in this matter ever having been filed with the EDC as required by statute."

"Mr. Public Advocate, please! Technicalities. This man is killing the city on technicalities. Ever since he got here he's been stopping any chance of progress. That site was legally condemned. *That's* the law," Lasker screamed angrily.

A definite buzz overtook the room. Council members looked at each other and some could be heard asking each other, "What the fuck is going on?"

"There are also laws to protect the weak from the rich, and who entitled you to the river views anyway?" Calhoun responded heatedly.

Lasker went ballistic at the mention of rich.

"Who said that factory workers and illegal aliens are entitled to the best view of the New York skyline? They can work elsewhere. In America the bucks own the views! And rich! What rich? New York doesn't have any more rich. You've chased us all away. And what do you have to show for it? What are your credentials? You haven't built one office, one store. You're a nothing. A numbers man who got lucky catering to every goo-goo demonstrator with a petition!"

The public advocate's flustered eyes roved the room wildly; he rapped his gavel incessantly.

"Meeting adjourned. We're putting this over for executive session," he commanded without much conviction.

Lasker's lawyers pulled him away fuming from the confrontation, as the Meyers' employees cheered wildly. Kevin looked up to see the crowd racing toward him, screaming excitedly, while a smoldering Anselmo stared at him for a moment, executed a graceful Little Lord Fauntleroy bow and humming, walked slowly out of the chamber.

Calhoun was totally engulfed by Ben, Max, and the factory workers; Max and some of the women were in tears. The deputy mayor felt a joy which he had never experienced before in public life; Calhoun's career had finally intersected with life. A political technician was metamorphosing before everyone's eyes into a politician—his own public man.

Mayor Pappas was receiving thunderous applause for a speech he had just given to 1,000 members of the Catholic Youth movement at the Manhattan College Gymnasium, in the Riverdale section of the Bronx. He left the dais to subsequent speakers with a generous wave, in order to move on to his next public event, when George handed him a phone. Slipping behind the temporarily erected wooden stands, Mayor Pappas acknowledge his caller with a "thank you" and immediately dialed a number.

As Calhoun exulted in his new status, Sergeant-at-Arms Hanley signaled him toward a row of special phone booths reserved for Council members.

"It's the Mayor," Hanley said evenly, as he handed Calhoun the receiver.

"What happened?" Pappas inquired with

the concern of one who already had the facts and now sought the back story.

"The point is, what didn't happen?" the deputy mayor said jubilantly, still on his high.

"Okay, what didn't happen?" the mayor's voice expressed his annoyance at his deputy's immaturity.

"Councilman Frank Anselmo, political boss and the last of a dying breed, did not get his way," Calhoun gushed like a school girl.

"Frank Anselmo is not dying," the mayor said with a cold evenness. And after a moment's pause, he added, "Kevin, meet me at the BancExchange site."

"What time?"

"Now!" The mayor pressed the off button and handed the cellular phone to George.

Calhoun arrived at BancExchange and waited anxiously for the mayor, a tiny figure standing alone on acres of open waterfront lots and decaying piers encrusted with trash, broken bottles, and rusting car hulks. The Mayor's advance men pulled up and parked across the street adjacent to the largely deserted small factories and warehouses. And shortly thereafter the mayor arrived. He jumped out of the limousine and joined Kevin in the middle of a large lot. Both men stared in renewed awe across the lot at the magnificent Manhattan skyline.

"Well, what do you think?" the mayor inquired.

"What a view," Kevin replied brushing back the hair blowing in his face.

"A view! What a poet; what he sees is a view. The view is the least of it. This, my friend, is not a view, this is property surrounded by non-taxpaying abandoned buildings and small factories which could be relocated on land anywhere in the city. BancExchange can go forward. And nobody loses," Mayor Pappas said argumentatively.

"Thirty million dollars for a subway station, fifteen million dollars for an off-ramp, that's a lot of taxpayer money to bolster Lenny Lasker's property values," Kevin offered defensively.

"You tripped over the elephant while chasing a flea. Forget Frank Anselmo. Look at the long-term returns to those same taxpayers," the mayor said, with an implicit hint to reduce the pressure on Frank Anselmo.

"Frank Anselmo is not a flea," the deputy mayor replied, still savoring his victory over the ancient regime.

"Don't press the metaphor, all this is about is getting things done. I'm going to meet with Frank Anselmo myself. And he's going to give us the votes we need for BancExchange. He has a lock on them. When the train leaves the station, Kevin, you want to be aboard." He raised his voice instructively.

"But I thought you told me *no* on infrastructure," Kevin said, reminding him of their earlier conversation at Gracie Mansion.

The mayor winced at his Deputy's naivete.

"I said don't give him infrastructure, I never said, 'Don't give him BancExchange.' We, the City, need it."

Calhoun threw his hands into the air, expressing his frustration as Mayor Pappas continued with a rotating swivel of his hips. "Politics is about being effective. You should have adjusted, Kevin."

"How are you going to pay for it, Mr. Mayor?"

"We'll find a way," he said reassuringly. The mayor told an advance man to drive Kevin's car and invited his deputy mayor to join him in his limousine for the trip to City Hall.

CHAPTER THIRTEEN

New York Repertory Theatre's premiere of *Carousel* was a benefit on behalf of the Governor's Committee on Scholastic Achievement. For the City's political and media elite, this evening was the equivalent of opening night at the Metropolitan Opera for old-line high-society WASPs.

Seated in the surrounding darkness of a Lincoln Center performance, Mayor Pappas could justify to himself the loneliness and vulnerability of public service. "It's all worth it," he thought looking around at government's child, "if you can use that one big chance to make a difference."

Master public servant Robert Moses and billionaire philanthropist John D. Rockefeller built Lincoln Center on the bones of decaying tenement buildings through a public-private partnership. And they realized their dream of creating a cultural critical mass in Manhattan, which would be sufficient in its quality and diversity to continually attract universal audiences. The dying West Side metamorphosed into the cultural heartbeat of a world-class New York City. "Could BancExchange be a little, but not insignificant, chance to make a difference?" the Mayor reflected, while looking two rows in front of him at Anselmo and his wife Nettie.

Frank and Nettie held hands throughout the performance, and at several points both of them were reciting the lines along with the actors on stage. From time to time, Anselmo looked over and smiled at his wife or whispered something in her ear. As Billy Bigelow and Julie Jordan began singing "If I Loved You," in the reflected light Mayor Pappas could follow the trail of a single tear falling down Anselmo's eye and disappearing under his chin.

The Intel bodyguard seated just behind the Mr. and Mrs. Pappas leaned forward in response to the flick of his boss's index finger: "I want to see Frank Anselmo on the balcony. Right now," he ordered. Five minutes later the gentlemen were engaged in conversation on the windy balcony overlooking Lincoln Center Plaza, with its magnificent fountain, the Met with its Marc Chagall mural and Philharmonic Hall glowing in the background.

"We're missing the best part," complained Anselmo.

"You know it by heart anyway," Pappas said pinching his friend's fleshy cheek.

"Do you like the Billy Bigelow, John?"

"Good voice, no acting. How do you feel about the Julie Jordon?"

"Good act, no voice. My Nettie could sing better. When we met twenty-five years ago, she was singing in *Carousel* at the Westbury Music Circus," Anselmo said smiling in recollection.

"I remember; she was in the chorus. Nettie was something then . . . and now. Speaking of performances, Frank, I don't want to hear about another one like yesterday's from you."

"Your boy embarrassed me," Frank said in absolute justification.

"You should have kept talking. There's never a need for a public showdown." The mayor paused for a second, then: "There's oil under those vacant lots, Frank. *Urban* oil. Jobs!"

"Hey, I helped put BancExchange together. You don't need to politick me," Anselmo said, expressing a "who are you kidding attitude."

"Jobs. For the people of this city. Not leases for Lenny Lasker and all of your greedy pals," the mayor enjoined.

"You don't have jobs without development and that means leases and developers," Anselmo rejoined in genuine astonishment. "What's happened to you, John? Just because the kid thinks he can elect you president, are you going to forget who got you here?"

"You're developing a short memory, Frank. Or a very selective one," the mayor said, reminding Anselmo of the symbiotic nature of their relationship.

"I'm sorry," Frank responded with regret at arguing with his friend.

The mayor also felt the wastefulness of this encounter.

"Look, the subway stop costs me thirty million dollars, the off-ramp fifteen million. The City's budget can't take it. I have to beg it from Albany, and my other cups need more urgent filling right now," the mayor implored Frank for understanding.

"I got a solution. How about hitting up the Feds for an Amtrak spur?" Anselmo suggested jauntily.

"Don't be funny. At a hundred twenty million dollars a track mile, they won't pony up a nickel. Now you listen to me. BancExchange's good for the middle class. Good for the jobless.

Good for the whole goddamn city. As for the subway stop, off-ramps, infrastructure . . . stop already, we can't afford it," the mayor said testily.

"Then you're going to have to forget the whole thing. It's all about votes and I got the noses in the City Council," Frank replied matter-of-factly.

At that moment the doors flung open and the audience rolled out for intermission.

"I love the second act opener," Anselmo continued.

"It'll be coming up soon," the Mayor warned.

"Then let's not miss it," Anselmo said indicating his first susceptibility to compromise.

"Okay, here it is, Frank, take it or leave it. I'm building up my IOUs with Albany. By next year, the governor will have to step up for a new off-ramp—or I won't support him for reelection. And I'll budget half the funding for the subway stop in fiscal 1996 and half in 1997. You'll get it all, just have to wait awhile."

"Next year's too far away," Anselmo replied without much vigor.

"Remember, Frank, you're only a boss. I'm the mayor. Mayors rule." Pappas let the message sink in, with a pregnant pause, then went on: "BancExchange, Frank. My way or the highway!"

"Why do I get the feeling you get the bigger half?" Anselmo asked plaintively.

"Let me ask you something, Frank. If I'd offered you less, would you have been polite and taken it?" The mayor put warmth and mutual understanding into the remark rather than a challenge.

"Of course," Anselmo responded with laughter.

"Then you got what you wanted," Mayor Pappas said hugging his friend. And while they embraced, the mayor added, "There's one more thing."

"What is that?" Frank asked skeptically, as he gently pulled away.

"My economic development commissioner tells me it will take 3.5 million dollars to build Meyers a new factory at our College Point Industrial Park. It's not too far away and the same employees could work there. How much is Lasker paying, again?"

"He grabbed it for one million. I forced it up to two million," Anselmo said, alerting the mayor that it was no easy task.

"Let's make it 3.5 million dollars and you have the whole zoning envelope, plus infrastructure on our agreed terms. It's a package you can live with, Frank. And there are *no losers.*" Mayor Pappas emphasized the "no losers" like a political article of faith.

"Lasker will go nuts if I agree. John, we need him next year," Anselmo said, referring to the forthcoming campaign."

"Frank, this is a game of kings. Since when are the pawns dictating our moves? Let's do it clean, Frank."

Anselmo could feel the sincerity in the mayor's plea and knew that this request could be neither negotiated nor refused.

"Ah!" A big smile lit up Anselmo's face. "Lenny's the kind of scumbag who can always make ends meet." And Anselmo embraced his friend, planting a big kiss on his cheek. "I guess you're all grown up, my boy," Frank breathed in John's ear with pride.

The theater lights were flashing on and off to indicate the start of the second act. Just before Anselmo opened the door to the theater, Pappas grabbed his arm. "Answer me one question, Frank," he said. "You've seen this show a dozen times—"

Frank cut in: "A hundred times!"

"A hundred times, and it still makes you cry. You're a grown man. In fact, you're a tough son of a bitch. Why does goddamn *Carousel* make you bawl like a baby?" Both men stopped in their tracks for a moment.

"It isn't *just* the show, John, it's the situation. You're watching these people who seem very average. They're not kings or politicians or anything. Julie works in a mill and Billy's a big lug who's having trouble growing up. They're just trying to do the best they can from day to day. But we know the system is working against them, and Billy's working against himself. That they are doomed by his tragic flaws. They can't fight their fate. Billy thinks he's finally saved by falling in love and having a daughter. But we know he's going to be dead by the end of the act." Anselmo and the mayor stood perfectly still, staring at each other, separated by Intel bodyguards from the curious crowd pressing past them into the auditorium.

The mayor was deep in thought. "That's putting a lot of weight into a goddamn Broadway musical," he said. "You think all people have tragic flaws?"

"John, that is one thing your people and my people have in common. Spanish and Italians, we know all about tragic flaws. When destiny creates the circumstances in which these flaws must be played out, the curtain inevitably comes down," Anselmo replied with utmost seriousness.

"You think you and I are *doomed* by our tragic flaws?" Pappas asked playfully, punching his friend in the ribs.

Anselmo paused, before looking at his watch.

"Your Honor, I know one thing for sure," he said.

"Okay, I'll bite. What's the one thing you know for sure?"

Stepping through the doors into the crowded theater, Anselmo turned gently to Pappas and smiled with satisfaction. "I know for sure that this was a real nice clambake, and I'm mighty glad I came."

Pappas was still feeling the warm afterglow of an old friendship when Calhoun rushed up to him at the back of the theater. They stepped into the lobby, as the curtain came up. Calhoun was holding a drink in each hand.

"So BancExchange is a go?" Kevin asked excitedly.

"How'd you know?" Pappas asked.

"Along with half of New York I watched you smile and shake hands and embrace. Ruling out the announcement of an engagement, BancExchange seemed the next most likely explanation. So, how did you get him on board?"

"By not saying no. I just put him off on the infrastructure. And he'll get Lasker to pay Meyer's full cost of relocation to a brand-new factory."

"But that's a no. Lasker will take a bath."

"He'll get it back. And more. It'll just take a little more time. Something for him and something for me. That's how things get done."

"More for you, I hope," Calhoun said.

"More for the City," Pappas replied with a professional's smile. He pointed to the drinks Calhoun was holding. "I'm guessing one of those is for my wife."

"She was over there a minute ago," Calhoun said, pointing to a corner of the room that was empty now that most people had resumed their seats. "But now they're both for me. It will help Frank Anselmo go down."

Pappas shook his head from side to side as Calhoun downed the drinks one after the other. "I like a two-fisted drinker," the mayor remarked. "Maybe it will lighten you up."

Mayor Pappas' tone was almost playful, but Calhoun could feel the seriousness beneath his words.

"This is politics. Nothing more, nothing less. It's what we do. That includes you. But you want to pick and choose. You love the numbers kind of politics where you can deal with computers. But when you have to do the people kind of politics and deal with someone equal, like Frank, you don't like it. You want to pick up your toys and go home. I'll tell you like a father would tell you, Kevin, this is a flaw. You're treating it like a virtue and cultivating it. But, believe me, you should be treating it like a flaw and try to correct it. As one of your heroes, Harry Truman, said, 'If you can't stand *Carousel*, you should get out of the theater.' "

Kevin didn't wish to respond, so he changed the subject.

"I sent a draft of the eulogy for the Bone child up to the mansion with your overnight reading package," he said, very businesslike.

"Thanks," Pappas said, his voice suddenly very heavy.

CHAPTER FOURTEEN

The cops had hoped for a rainy day to keep the crowds indoors during Robby Bone's funeral procession. Instead this cold, bright day invited hundreds of stone-silent mourners to follow behind Robby Bone's hearse, which moved slowly from Carver Houses to Grace Church. Edgar Bone led the procession with a slow, mechanical shuffle, leaning leadenly on his elderly father, who had his arm wrapped tightly around his forlorn child in support and hopeless rage. Bone's once shiny ebony face was now discolored and desolate with the grim reality that his son was gone, lost to him forever.

Thousands more watched the procession

from sidewalks, their faces mirroring a shared feeling of quiet indignation that a great crime had been committed against this community. Occasional clusters of youths raised their fists into the air in disembodied futile defiance of a world they couldn't comprehend.

A big choir positioned in the balcony, wearing black silk robes with brilliant scarlet trim, greeted the mourners as they filed into the small church. As Edgar Bone and his father carried their deep hurt down the central aisle, a soloist began singing an old spiritual:

"What then? What then?
When the great Book is opened, what then?
And a world that rejected its Savior
Will be asked for a reason.
What then?"

"But why must those like Bone, who had not sinned, have to pay the price for the sinners?" Calhoun couldn't help wondering, as he stood on the side of the church, awaiting the mayor's eulogy.

Wails overtook the spiritual as a small, white coffin was slowly wheeled in. Grief-stricken relatives reached out to touch it, as if they could somehow let Robby know how deeply he was loved and how sorely he was missed.

Mayor Pappas was standing to the far right of the altar, between Deputy Police Commissioner Melvin Sanders, the highest-ranking black officer in the NYPD, and the Reverend Leonard Chapman, Pastor of Grace Church. Sanders leaned over to give Mayor Pappas a final briefing.

"We've got heavy surveillance and no one gets into the church without a heavy eyeball by at least a couple of our men who know this area and know who the players are. But we haven't dared use a metal detector, so we can't be sure that . . ." His voice trailed off but the his look spoke louder than his words. "Stand high on the altar, way back from the coffin!"

"Any trouble along the procession route?" Pappas asked.

"Quiet. We haven't really heard from any of the usual rabble-rousers."

"Good," Pappas affirmed. "But sometimes the offense is so great that the rabble is roused all by itself."

"Yes sir, and those are the most dangerous. When you don't know how to make plans for it," Sanders said, casting his eyes over the seated crowd.

The NYPD had experience with smoldering ghetto rage, the silence of smoke that could erupt into conflagration at the slightest unpredictable provocation, turning a mourning crowd into a deadly mob instantaneously.

"You're sure Reverend Chapman will introduce me?" the mayor asked, somewhat as an undeserving supplicant.

"Yes sir, right at the beginning, before the service begins, but only with a single sentence."

"And when I'm finished?"

"We get out of here."

"Which way?" the mayor inquired, and the police chief pointed his finger to a side door.

The mayor shook his head. "No," he said firmly. "The front. The mayor must go out the front."

Pastor Chapman walked to the pulpit in his funeral robe of black silk with magnificently embroidered purple. The choir passionately sang its final verse.

"What then? What then?
When the great Book is opened, what then?
And the Savior comes again in judgment,
And we stand up before Him,
What then?"

Pastor Chapman stood, his head bowed in silent prayer, until the last echo of the song had disappeared. When he looked up, his gaze first fell upon the coffin in the middle of the aisle directly beneath him. His face was brimming with sadness for his flock. The pastor's eyes swept across the congregation, momentarily meeting familiar souls with compassion, healing their wounds, comforting their doubts, breaking the terrible tension engulfing his beloved church. Finally he spoke, his voice deep and warm.

"Sisters, brethren . . . the Mayor of the City of New York, the Honorable John Pappas."

Despite the earlier warning from Sanders, the mayor was still shocked by the terseness of his introduction. Behind the pulpit he felt the enormous emotional void, which had to be filled, and he knew that the standard condolences and prayer Calhoun had prepared for him would not do. But what could he say?

The mayor's eyes locked into the lifeless orbs of a formless panther in the front pew. For a small instant the mayor stood motionless, staring into Edgar Bone's crushed soul, washed over by memories of losing his own son, when his own heart was drowned in sorrow and death could come only as a relief. Then he looked at the mourners, their hearts sinking in grief, without a breath of hope in the room. John Pappas felt their eyes looking toward God, begging for a sign of hope in the next life; he knew instinctively that he had to raise the window of hope at least slightly for them in this life and he started to speak extemporaneously.

"What then? The spiritual asks us—what then? What then when the cities run to sewers and the lights are extinguished and the officials corrupt? What then when the streets are no longer safe, and when a father holds his child by the hand, and the boy is cut down and cast aside like chaff in the field, what then?"

As he paused, a single voice from the middle of the congregation spoke out: "Say it plain!"

"People warned me. They said, 'Don't stand behind the coffin. You don't dare to stand behind the coffin.' But how can I heed their warning when a heartbeat is silent—and a child is dead?"

Looking directly at Edgar Bone, Pappas stepped down from the pulpit and onto the floor of the church. As he moved toward the coffin, some angry murmurs spread through the pews. The ushers looked concerned, and the police were tensed for action. The mayor seemed oblivious and continued talking, almost as if to himself, as he approached Robby Bone.

" 'Don't stand behind that coffin,' they said, because that little boy was as pure and innocent as the driven snow. But I must stand here, and I am by no means innocent, and by the time this winter's snow touches the ground under my feet, it will turn as gray and gritty as the stones of hell."

Sincerity from deep personal pain in the mayor's voice, and in his movement, seemed to reach out to touch the shared suffering in the congregation. Several voices called out, "Yes!" Someone else shouted, "Go on!"

"But can I tell you something," Pappas asked, looking around the room. "Will you allow me this? I feel I am this boy. I am Robby Bone. Oh yes, he lies there and I stand here. He is gone and I survive, but can I tell you, my soul is crushed, my spirit wanting because I have let you down. I have died on you because I have not given you the protection you crave, the safe homes you cherish, the streets to transport yourselves.

"That is no city. Not for you. Not for me. We have no city until we can walk abroad and recreate ourselves. Until we can stroll the streets like boulevards and congregate in parks with joy, our families mingle, our children laugh, our hearts joined. Label me a failure until that day comes. But take my hand now, won't you? Trust me for one perilous moment, will you not? Together we can find the path, we'll rebuild together, and the en-

gine for our efforts will be this child, his spirit,
his innocence, his memory.

"Can I do it? Can I come back from this?"

The room suddenly seemed to come alive,
as if an electric current had suddenly passed
through the church. Calhoun and Sanders exchanged incredulous glances as Pappas, seeming to gain strength from the mourners,
continued to speak.

"I shall! And I will!" he shouted. The congregation, partially released from its frozen
agony, met his shout with their own. "Tell the
truth!" "Praise God!" "Yes we will!"

"Were we not great once and could we not
be great again? I put that question to Edgar
Bone, and his only answer is silence. I have
failed him and I have failed you. I know that.
But could not something pass from this sweet
youth to me, could he not empower me to
find the strength, to have the knowledge, to
summon up the courage to accomplish the
task?"

The mayor was totally absorbed in the moment. One could feel all of John Pappas' emotions galvanize in his words, as he raised his
right arm and repeatedly pressed it forward in
a rocking spear-throwing motion, almost
chanting:

"Yes, this is the palace that was the City. A
palace in which there is no king, no duke, no

prince, but only subjects beholden to each other to make a better place to live. We will do it. We will rebuild on the soul of this little warrior. I am with you, little Robby, I *am* you, and I will carry your bright standard forward until the palace that was the City rises once again. Yes! I choose to fight, I choose to fight, fight until this City, your City, our City is a palace again."

The mayor leaned over and kissed the little coffin. The entire room was on its feet, praying and praising God. The Intel men watched their worst nightmare unfolding before their eyes, as the entire congregation spilled into the aisles, with the mayor slowly working his way through it. He walked the length of the center aisle alone on his way to the front of the church. Calhoun and the Intel detachment had looped around the side aisle and met the mayor just as he reached the street door. Forming a phalanx around him, they emerged onto the church's front steps.

The mayor's words had been broadcast on the loudspeakers outside the church. A hundred uniformed police and scores of plainclothes tensed themselves to be ready for whatever came next. The crowd stood more sad then angry, as Mayor Pappas passed through it. The loudspeakers carried the choir's words out onto the street.

"I want to dig a little deeper
Yes dig a little deeper
I want to dig a little deeper
In the storehouse of God's love!"

An old black lady prayed repeatedly, as the mayor moved by her. "God bless you, God bless you," she said over and over. Catching her words, the mayor stopped, touched her tiny shoulders with both hands and in a humble, painfully naked voice simply said, "Thank you, thank you so much."

An exhausted Mayor Pappas sprawled out, eyes closed, in the limousine.

"That was a fine speech, Mr. Mayor," Kevin said admiringly.

"That was nothing," Pappas responded hollowly. "God is playing a sick joke on me. I came into office wanting to help those people; and now I'm giving funeral orations, while burying their children."

CHAPTER FIFTEEN

Zapatti felt at home in his Gravesend Hunting and Fishing Club. Practically speaking it was as secure as the Pentagon war room. Thick steel doors, which were positioned at intervals along a terraced staircase, remained sealed unless opened from inside by a different soldier with a specific code for each lock. The walls and ceilings were reinforced to resist intrusion and sensitive alarms provided early warning of even the most feeble attempt at penetration. Expensive electronic counter-measures, augmented by daily human sweeps, guarded against eavesdropping and camera surveillance. Finally, to prevent the FBI from disabling the electricity which sustained his fortress, Zapatti had heavy portable generators that kicked in when the juice from outside got too low.

Lenny Lasker was a snake between mongooses, trying to act like he was enjoying lunch at the club with Paul Zapatti and Frank Anselmo. "Jesus, this is great," he said, uneasily turning his fork in the red-hot pasta putanesca heaped in front of him.

"I hired the chef from Rao's kitchen in Manhattan. You got to feed your crew good," Zapatti said with a condescending smile.

Lenny waited for the small talk about food to abate and jumped into the opening with a subject burning a hole right through his stomach.

"I don't understand how you guys are so calm," he said, trying to keep his own rage under control, "seeing that the mayor has left us holding the bag."

Because Lasker kept his eyes firmly fixed on a fat black olive sticking out of the red mess he made of his putanesca, he missed the look of utter dismissive disgust which shot between the eyes of Anselmo and Zapatti.

"But, Lenny," Anselmo said patiently, as if addressing a child, "the bag we're holding is full of cash."

"Minus a year and plus 3.5 million dollars in cost," Lasker said, unwilling to be appeased.

"But you can weather a year, Lenny," Anselmo said, his voice even more soothing than before. "You could weather a hundred years. You're holding so many deep in the money options on land in this town that you could *buy* Queens."

But Lenny Lasker was not to be placated. "I got partners," he said truculently. "What's the matter with you guys? *You're* my partners."

"That's right, Lenny," Anselmo continued, "and I'm the one who took the shot in the City Council. I'm the guy who got my ass handed to me in front of my colleagues and my constituents and anyone who happens to own a TV set. Image is power. So if I'm not whining, why should you?"

"I'm not whining," Lasker complained.

"Of course you're not," Zapatti said. "Now, Lenny, if you don't mind—and if you're finished eating—Frank and I have something we have to discuss privately."

The men watched as Lenny Lasker's brain balanced his relief at not having to pretend to eat his putanesca anymore with his resentment at being dismissed in the middle of the meal. After a few tortuous seconds, relief necessarily won out, and Lenny pushed his chair back.

"Sure, sure, Paul. No sweat. In fact, I got an

important appointment uptown," Lenny said just a trifle too grandly.

"Then it works out nicely," Zapatti replied drily.

The men rose and Anselmo put his arm around Lenny's shoulder. "Lenny, just remember the saying: Everything comes to he who waits. So we just have to wait, and everything will come. Okay?" Anselmo said, summoning up as reasonable a tone as his irritation would allow.

"Okay, Frank, okay," Lasker said with the conviction of a general whose own weapons were pointing at him.

When he had gone, both men sighed at having to put up with an unwelcome guest. "Just goes to prove you can have seven hundred million dollars and still be an asshole," Anselmo said, laughing. "If he doesn't watch his mouth, someone will cut him a new asshole for free," Zapatti added.

Both men were silent as the waiter arrived to clear the plates and bring them each a double espresso.

"Are we really sure that BancExchange is all set?" Zapatti asked.

"Absolutely," Anselmo affirmed. "We got everything we wanted, with a slight delay and Lasker paying a reasonable relocation fee."

"*Bene, multo bene.* Now there is something

else you can do for me, Frank," Zapatti said offhandedly.

"Anything, Paul. Just ask."

"Get my name out of the papers," the mafia boss responded forcefully.

"Yeah, right," Anselmo said chuckling nervously. The media was having a heyday with this story. That morning's *New York Post* headline had been "Cop on Zapatti's Hit List?"

"Frank, I'm not kidding about this," Zapatti said.

Anselmo experienced a sinking feeling as he realized his friend was perfectly serious. "But how?" he asked.

"With forty thousand dollars," Zapatti said.

"But, Paul, this story is dynamite. Forty thousand wouldn't even buy off the *Rego Park Pennysaver* for Christ's sake," Anselmo protested.

Zapatti smiled without satisfaction. "Let me ask you a question," he said. "Have you ever heard of a cop with forty thousand?"

"Yes, sure," Anselmo replied tentatively.

"Who wasn't crooked?"

"No," was the answer.

"Everybody's got a bug up his ass about some pissant probation report," Zapatti said contemptuously. "They're ignoring the real problem."

"Police corruption," Anselmo supplied.

"Of course." Zapatti nodded vigorously.

"Takes the spotlight off me and puts it where it ought to be. Santos was a dirty cop, like so many in the ghetto precincts, who got blown away trying to extract payoffs. Good riddance, as far as the public is concerned."

"But Paul, we've already got problems because something didn't stay fixed," Anselmo pleaded. "We ought to just wait this thing out. Things could get really messy now that everybody is all over this goddamn thing."

"Things *are* really messy already, Frank, and I want my problem taken care of now. Capice?"

"I understand," Anselmo replied without enthusiasm.

"I knew you would, Frank." Zapatti downed his espresso and put a manila envelope on the table between them continuing, "I knew I could count on you. Give my best to Nettie." As he left with a wave, three hulking men materialized from the bar to form a phalanx around him.

For what seemed like several moments, Anselmo sat uneasily sipping from his empty espresso cup. Finally, he moved the manila envelope to the seat of the chair next to him. It was only closed by its folded-down metal clasp. He could feel four separate stacks, each secured with a rubber band, and each containing, he knew without even having to look, ten thousand dollars.

CHAPTER SIXTEEN

The weather was threatening to change. The sun had risen in a brilliant blue sky, but by eight o'clock the sky had turned a solid gunmetal gray, and a bitter wind began to blow close to the ground. A lone bagpiper detached himself from the police department band and stood at the top of the little hill just beyond an open grave. The last mournful notes of "Amazing Grace" floated through the freezing air.

Kevin Calhoun looked across the open grave at Eddie's flag-draped casket and then to Elaine Santos. A black veil hid her face, but he could see from the shaking of her shoulders beneath a thin black coat that she was crying.

Her sister stood next to her, holding the hands of Elaine's two children—babies really, and luckily too little to understand anything except that something terrible had happened to Daddy, that Daddy had gone away.

Hundreds of uniformed police stood at attention; each with a strip of black tape across his badge; each face stern, each far too accustomed to this kind of occasion.

Police Commissioner Coogan was finishing up his brief eulogy. He wasn't a very good speaker, but Coogan was so clearly touched by the tragedy that had befallen one of his men, that his words carried a certain power. "We need heroes so badly," he said, "that we are grateful to have had one like Eddie Santos, even if it was for far too short a time." He paused and nodded at Calhoun. Calhoun stepped forward and bowed his head. Keeping his eyes on the casket; he spoke softly. "Mayor Pappas deeply regrets that duty forces him to be two hundred fifty miles away in Washington right now, but he is also right here, standing with us, saying good-bye to a brave man who gave his life in the line of duty. Eddie Santos was still so young. He should be as he was before—arriving at the precinct, bursting with energy, ready to start the day fighting criminals. Or he should be rushing home to his beautiful young wife and two magnificent

children, full of love, full of promise. There is
no point in trying to make sense of the mad-
ness that brings us to this sad place. We resolve to remember Eddie's energy and love;
and to honor his commitment to his job and
to this City. We will remember Eddie, and we
will honor Eddie. But most of all, we will
miss Eddie."

The bagpiper began playing some new and
even more mournful tune. The drums of the
police band, muffled with funeral black, struck
a solemn beat. Suddenly, the sky seemed filled
with thunder as five police helicopters zoomed
overhead, with one place vacant in their formation. Eddie's daughter, Lisa, pointed excitedly to the choppers. She squeezed Elaine's
hand and asked, "Mommy, Mommy, are they
taking Daddy to heaven?"

The coffin was slowly lowered into the
ground. "Man, thou art dust and unto dust
you shall return," intoned the department
chaplain. He took the gold crucifix from the
top of the coffin and gently handed it to Linda.
The five-year-old stared quizzically at the
shiny object, while her three-year-old sister
watched her enviously, wondering why nothing was given to her.

The mourners started filing past Elaine, who
raised her veil so she could look each one in
the eye. The last in line was the deputy mayor.

"Thanks for the words," she said quietly.

"It's the least we can do," Kevin replied.

Suddenly Marybeth Cogan stepped along-side Elaine Santos. "Good morning, Mr. Cal-houn," she said coldly. "Where is the mayor?"

"He had to be in Washington this morning," Calhoun answered.

"A detective killed in the line of duty rates an inspector's funeral, and that includes the mayor," she stated.

"Let me assure you, the mayor's absence in no way diminishes his concern for Mrs. Santos and her children," Calhoun said as civilly as he could manage. He handed Elaine Santos his card.

"Mrs. Santos," he said, "if there's anything I can do, please call me."

As if a dam had burst, Elaine Santos grabbed Calhoun's arm. "Where do they get that stuff in the newspapers?" she asked, straining to hold back the tears. "The kids at school, they tell my son that his daddy was a drug dealer."

"I'm very sorry," Calhoun said. "We'll do everything we can to stop the speculation. We'll put our press people on it right away."

Marybeth was implacable. "What about In-ternal Affairs?" she asked. "What are those clowns doing here?" Calhoun followed her gaze. At the edge of the crowd, two men with short haircuts and ill-fitting overcoats were openly watching the departing mourners.

"I'm sure they're just here to pay their respects," Calhoun said without much conviction. Marybeth gave him a withering look as she led Elaine and the children to their limousine.

As Calhoun drove his Jeep through the gates of the cemetery, he saw Marybeth Cogan standing in front of the Plexiglas bus shelter on Fresh Meadow Lane. He pulled over and opened the passenger's side window.

"Where are you going?" he called out.

She looked at him disdainfully. "Where do you think?" she replied. "I'm taking a bus back to the city."

"I thought we were in the city," he said gamely.

"Not if you're from Queens," she stated.

Still leaning across the seat, with his foot on the brake, he said, "Let's start over, okay? Where are you going?"

"Manhattan."

"So hop in."

"Go fuck yourself," she said, and was immediately surprised at herself. "No, I'm sorry," she said, "that was rude, and I'm sorry."

Calhoun shrugged. "No harm done," he said.

She looked down the busy road, as if willing the bus to appear.

"You know you could wait here for an hour." Leaning over again, he said, "Come on, you don't have to talk to me, and you'll be back at work at least two hours earlier than if you wait here."

He had been prepared for further hesitation, but she surprised him by entering. He realized that the seat was covered with newspapers, legal pads, and empty plastic coffee cups. She gracefully held herself suspended in air while he swept everything onto the floor.

"How are you going to go?" she asked as soon as they had turned into traffic.

"Well," he said, "I thought I'd take the LIE."

"I hate the Long Island Expressway," she said. "Take the Grand Central. It's much better. You'll catch it at Astoria Boulevard."

"I know where I could catch it," he said, and they lapsed into silence.

They drove along the broad boulevards of the borough of Queens. For dozens of blocks it seemed as if every other business was either an auto parts store, a cellular telephone shop, or a small family restaurant. Marybeth finally turned to Calhoun. "He was a good cop, you know. Eddie Santos was a good cop. And either you're doing a vile thing or you're allowing a vile thing to be done."

"You keep saying that," Calhoun protested, "but nobody's doing anything."

"You've got all the answers, don't you? she said, sneering.

"Miss Cogan, I don't even have the questions yet."

When they were stopped at a red light, she turned to him and said, "Okay, I have a question for you."

"Shoot."

"You hungry?"

"You serious?"

"Yes."

"I'm starved."

"So am I. How would you like a Philly steak sandwich?" Before Calhoun could respond, she said, "Quick, swing by that diner over there—the NorthStar. They make the best Philly steak sandwiches in New York City. Or, as you would probably call them, Philadelphia steak sandwiches."

Calhoun smiled as he jockeyed the Jeep across two lanes of traffic.

"You're in for a real treat," Marybeth said as she unfastened her seat belt. Calhoun didn't move. "Aren't you coming in?" she asked.

"Not until you fill me in on exactly what the hell you're doing," he said sternly.

"What exactly do you mean?"

"What I mean, exactly," he said mocking

her tone, "is that although I can't stop you from insulting my character, I can stop you from insulting my intelligence. I know the NorthStar and its specialties very well, and I know that, while you have strong feelings about many things, one of them is not the Long Island Expressway."

"What are you talking about? she persisted.

"You were waiting for me at the bus stop, looking sufficiently fetching and sufficiently forlorn to be sure I'd stop," he said. "And we both know that the Grand Central Parkway is the long way around. So, what I'm talking about is, who the hell are we going to meet in there?"

Without hesitation she said, "We're going to meet Detective Albert Holly. He and Eddie were partners two years ago when Tino Zapatti walked."

Calhoun quickly processed the information. "Thank you," he said, as he undid his seat belt and opened the car door.

The deputy mayor was introduced to Detective Holly.

"Which precinct you in?" Calhoun asked.

"Fifty-first, City Island," Holly replied without energy. "The department put me there for healing."

While they waited for their Philly steak sandwiches, a despairing and clearly burnt-out Holly told them about his former partner. "Eddie was a pitbull," Holly said both admiringly and regretfully, given the result.

"Pitbulls are ugly, but they're not stupid," Calhoun said bluntly. "What was he doing without a backup?"

"It wasn't the first time he'd taken Tino down, only he never had a problem with him before," Holly said, and he sounded genuinely confused by this detail of Eddie Santos' last moments. "I don't know. Tino must have gotten the drop on him. It happens."

"Shit happens," Calhoun agreed, "but why didn't Santos let anybody else know he was going up there?"

"Eddie probably felt his superiors wouldn't let him go after a judge. So it became *his* collar. You know, an obsession," Holly said. "He had made an airtight case against Tino and then that judge let Tino walk. Eddie went so crazy when he heard the sentence that I practically had to tie him down in the hallway. The whole thing stank. There is no way Tino Zapatti could have walked unless the judge was in somebody's pocket."

"Walter Stern has a national reputation," Calhoun stated.

"See, that's what Eddie faced." After a pause, Holly continued. "I don't give a shit if he's Oliver Wendell Holmes," Holly said contemptuously. "Somebody got to him. Or above him. I knew it and Eddie knew it. We were both pissed off. The difference between Eddie and me was he got nuts and wouldn't let go of it. Just like a pitbull. Not me. I was willing to do what I was obviously supposed to do: I went back to the precinct to disappear. So here we are, two years later. Eddie got five helicopters flying overhead and that's very impressive. On the other hand, he's six feet under, and that's very depressing."

Holly belched softly. "They didn't grill the onions and peppers first," he said, apologetically.

"They're less Philly than South Jersey," Marybeth agreed.

Calhoun had no interest in reviewing the food. "I'm going to want to get back to you," he said to Holly.

"Whoa," Holly protested. "Please don't get back to me. Please forget we ever met."

"What the hell is going on here?" Calhoun asked, looking from Holly to Marybeth.

"Don't make the same mistake as Eddie," Holly said to Calhoun. "Let it go. Let it lie. You're making a big mistake if you think you can finish what Eddie tried to start." Turning to Marybeth, he said, "And you, back off. Leave me alone. I've told you all I'm going to tell anybody. This here is my last public appearance on this topic. And if you take my advice, you'll stay far away from this one too. *Far away.*" He belched again and said goodbye.

CHAPTER SEVENTEEN

Judge Stern was presiding over a murder trial when Calhoun entered his near empty courtroom. The hulking, long-haired defendant hung his head on the table in front of him, with huge hands pressed firmly against his ears, while his lawyer laconically laid out a defense to the murder and cannibalization of a twenty-six-year-old female whom he picked up at a bar, stabbed thirty-eight times, and decapitated before eating her boiled parts. The public defender called a psychologist to support the defendant's claim that he killed the girl in accordance with meticulous instructions from God, who appeared to him in the form of a large shepherd hound incessantly barking orders into his ears. A handful of elderly trial junkies, who virtually inhabited the criminal courtrooms, muttered disapprovingly and were brought to order with a gavel rap by Judge Stern.

The defendant started to bark aggressively at the young prosecutor, who droned on with an objection over calling the witness. Two large uniformed guards moved in on him to protect the dignity of this proceeding.

"Where are you going with this, Mr. McKenar?" Judge Stern asked the prosecutor.

"The witness interprets the defendant's VA record one way, our psychologist interprets it another," the prosecutor responded in a monotone.

During this debate Calhoun walked down the center aisle to a low wooden barrier, separating the formal judicial proceedings area from the empty rows reserved for spectators. He handed a note to the court officer, who in turn handed it off to the judge's law clerk, who after a glance stretched his arm to hand the note up to Judge Stern on the bench. Stern looked over the courtroom at Calhoun, who nodded politely. The judge returned his attention to the proceedings.

"So much for expert witness," Stern interjected. "Each one interprets the same evidence one way, and another, and another until the end of time. I'll consider the objection in my chambers. Let's take a break, two-thirty all right for everybody?" And without waiting for a response, he rapped the gavel and left the bench, nodding to his clerk, Peter Ragan, who beckoned Calhoun to follow him into the judge's chambers.

As Ragan led the deputy mayor back to the Judge's chambers, he expressed his deep concern. "This is really a tragedy, Mr. Calhoun," the clerk said softly. "Judge Stern is the most cautious and conscientious jurist you could imagine, and this whole controversy is taking a lot out of him. Although he doesn't say anything, I know that Mr. Bone's vigil and circumstances are just tearing him apart," Ragan said knocking on a door bearing a plastic nameplate: JUDGE WALTER STERN.

"Come in, come in," Walter Stern said heartily as Ragan ushered Calhoun into the judge's chambers.

Calhoun was somewhat shocked by how small and unimpressive the room was, especially in contrast with the stature and affect naturally projected by its distinguished occupant. A battered desk, a couple of scarred chairs, and a dented steel filing cabinet were the only furniture. The flatness of this Spartan scene was accented only by a photograph of Stern with his grandchildren and another of him as a young clerk with Supreme Court Justice Hugo Black.

"The majesty of the law isn't expressed by its physical surroundings, Mr. Calhoun," Stern said with a tired smile. The judge followed Calhoun's eyes to the picture of him as a law clerk, and he added, "I'm sure it's hard to believe—I know Peter has a lot of trouble with the concept—but I was actually young once myself." His smile gave way to a flustered sadness and then formality. "But Mr. Calhoun, please forgive me. Have you been introduced to Peter Ragan, my law clerk? This man has written some of my best opinions. He appeared before me the first time I presided over the moot court at NYU, and you might say that we've been joined at the hip ever since."

"Yes, Your Honor, we met outside," Calhoun replied, but he shook hands with Ragan again in recognition of such a formal glowing introduction. Ragan immediately said he had some papers to research for the pending motion, and within a moment the door was closing behind him.

"Mr. Calhoun, please sit down," Stern said waving to one of the beat-up chairs facing his desk. "I won't pretend that I can't guess the reason for this visit," the judge continued calmly, "but I'm not sure exactly what I can do to help you."

Calhoun looked at Stern evenly and said, "Judge, you can tell me how Tino Zapatti got off with probation."

Stern did not reveal any surprise or discomfort at Calhoun's question or his manner. "I can only sentence in accordance with the conviction," he said simply. "Mr. Zapatti was convicted of criminal possession in the fourth degree."

"They found a kilo and a gun in his car—which was parked outside the schoolyard where he was doing business, Your Honor," Calhoun replied.

"Is it your intention to retry the case, Mr. Calhoun?" the judge inquired.

"There was a rap sheet a mile long," Calhoun persisted.

"Mr. Calhoun. I am certified in the State of New York as a Justice of the Supreme Court. You're sitting here rearguing a two-year-old case. I've come to expect it in the tabloids, but coming from you I find it improper in the extreme. And I shall inform the mayor of what you're doing."

"I'm here on the mayor's behalf," Calhoun said simply.

Judge Stern was finally visibly ill at ease. "Well then," he sputtered while trying to regain his composure, "why didn't anyone notify me that you were coming?"

"I'm sorry, Judge, but we thought it would be best if this were kept as low-keyed as possible. We're all friends, and we're just trying to figure out what's the best thing to do in a very difficult situation. We thought you might be able, and that you might be willing, to help us."

Walter Stern appeared to deflate before Calhoun's eyes. His chest sank and his shoulders seemed to cave under the sudden weight of his weary head. He pointed to a thin folder on the desk in front of him. Reading upside down, Calhoun could see the writing on the tab: ZAPATTI, TINO. "Do you think I've slept since this thing started?" the judge asked softly. "And can you even begin to imagine what it's like having Mr. Bone following me around everywhere I go, like the ghost at Banquo's table? And do you, for one minute, think I don't realize what a mistake I made?"

Calhoun could see that the judge was embarrassed by the desperation that had suddenly overtaken him; and he observed how strung out the gentleman was before he finally regained his regular voice.

"You see, Mr. Calhoun, there are certain guidelines," Judge Stern said. "I just don't make up laws as I go along. Quite the contrary, the genius of the law is that almost every situation under the sun has already been covered by it. I have guidelines," he said, once again almost defiant. "Have you forgotten the symbol of justice, Mr. Calhoun? It's two scales. And scales are for weighing. So, on the one hand, I had to weigh the fact that I was dealing with a potentially dangerous felon. But on the other hand, I had to weigh the fact that it was a low-class first conviction accompanied by a strongly positive probation report. And the guideline is perfectly clear. On a first conviction with a probation recommendation, the felon should go free under close supervision."

Calhoun waited for something else, something insightful. But Judge Stern only pushed the closed file to the side of his desk. "I was wrong," he said bluntly. "But there's nothing that you or I—or the mayor—can do to change that now."

Calhoun pushed his chair back. "Then I won't waste Your Honor's time," he said stiffly. Judge Stern either missed or was determined not to notice the coldness in Calhoun's tone. "You must forgive the surroundings," the judge said absent-mindedly, as he walked Calhoun to the door. "Courtrooms are grand, but behind the scenes, municipal gothic not only permeates the atmosphere, but sometimes creeps into the judicial system as well.

Judge Stern extended his hand. "Please accept my thanks, Mr. Calhoun, and please extend my warmest regards to the mayor. I just wish there was more I could do to help you," he said with a distracted shrug of his black-robed shoulders. And he stepped back into the trial, as Calhoun made a frustrated exit.

CHAPTER EIGHTEEN

Elaine Santos stood helplessly as Captain Florian of Internal Affairs brought shame to every ihch of Eddie's pride, his neat two-bedroom home on a quiet street in Hollis, Queens. Florian seemed to enjoy Elaine's tormented looks while he terrorized her with his hands crawling snakelike through Eddie's drawers. The widow's world was turned upside down. She had instantaneously plunged from secure wife of a hero detective to naked victim of the police department. Elaine was accustomed to being around men like her husband, who saw the world strictly in terms of good or evil, black and white, the law versus criminals; but in Florian she detected only darkness.

"You satisfied?" she finally cried out. "Did you find Eddie's million dollars, or his stash of coke, or whatever else your sick minds have invented for us?" Elaine continued contemptuously.

"Is there a basement?" Florian asked, showing no emotion.

"You saw it, the rumpus room," she responded.

"The knotty pine with the pool table?" he nudged her in a seemingly calculated attempt to agitate Elaine.

"That's right, Captain."

"Mrs. Santos, I'm only doing my job. I really am sorry," he said without real feeling.

"Sorry, crap! You're snooping around Eddie's house like a Nazi," she hollered.

"Please, you know this is the last thing I wanted to do," he replied hollowly.

"Then why don't you get the hell out of Internal Affairs and get yourself an honest job?" she screamed.

Elaine was fighting the anger and fatigue accumulated from her nights without end spent alone, worrying about the horrors she faced with her two young children entering a very cloudy future. The despair which accompanies feeling isolated in the clutches of an enemy who has life-and-death control over you was beginning to overtake Elaine when the phone rang. She walked slowly to the alcove between the kitchen and dining room to answer it. For a small moment Elaine fixated on dirty smudges covering the white handset, realizing that Eddie's fingers must have left them there just last weekend.

"Hello," she uttered shakily, tears streaming down her olive cheeks. Florian positioned himself in the dining room, so he could overhear the conversation. "Oh, I'm so glad to hear a friendly voice, Marybeth," Elaine said loudly for Florian's benefit. She felt a little more secure with Marybeth there to protect Eddie's pension and reputation, although deep down she didn't have much hope knowing that the whole system was working against her. "Yeah, Two Bars has been in here all morning. He's gone over the place from top to bottom," she continued. "No, of course he won't tell me what he's looking for. He's IA," Elaine responded to Marybeth's query.

As Florian listened to Elaine's conversation with her Detective Endowment Association lawyer, he spotted a photograph on the wall that caught his interest. It was a framed snapshot of Eddie and Elaine, with an older couple, in front of a modest cabin on the shore of what looked like a lake. Captain Florian turned it over and tried to decipher the faded handwriting on the cardboard back: "LAKE KERHONKSON, OCTOBER 8, 1991."

As Florian rehung the photo, Elaine continued with a desperate plea to Marybeth: "You've got to do something about Eddie's pension. They're going to try and take it away by labeling Eddie a rogue cop."

Elaine hung up and walked through the house. It was eerily empty, although she could still detect Florian's alien body odor infecting its pores, when she heard his car pull away from the curb.

The late winter sun was setting by the time the police reached the Santos' summer cabin outside Kerhonkson, New York, with about a dozen vehicles, representing the half-dozen jurisdictions involved in the raid. Strapping, starched New York State Troopers wearing Smoky the Bear hats stood alongside slouching long-haired NYPD detectives wearing rumpled suits. They smoked cigarettes while they watched their Crime Scene Unit, three men and two women wearing lurid orange jumpsuits with CSU in big black block letters emblazoned across their backs, busy at work tearing the place apart. One half of the two-member Kerhonkson Police Department arrived with the first wave of officers, and the other half arrived, with his kid brother in the passenger seat, about ten minutes later. Also present, but unacknowledged, were two members of the FBI's Organized Crime Unit.

Working in the deepening twilight, the CSU set up harsh halogen lamps. Every tree and bush along the innocent lakeside was suddenly stripped of its shadows and stood out in guilty-looking, unadorned relief. The CSU technicians continued to turn the modest cabin and its surroundings inside out. Every board of wood and every blade of grass was examined, labeled, and put back ever so slightly out of place.

A premeditated leak to the press had resulted in a media armada of cars and vans descending on the tranquil scene. Since none of the conflicting authorities was exactly in charge, the media roamed around relatively unsupervised. Forbidden any facts, the natural competition among reporters fueled the most extreme speculation concerning the reasons for the search and exactly what it was intended to uncover.

About three hours later, after the front yard and the porch had been torn up and the search had moved inside the house, the orange jumpsuits emerged exchanging significant looks and carrying a small, scarred metal box.

Well beyond the circle of light was yet another unmarked car, with a solitary occupant. Its occupant was the kind of man who loved plots, traps and black ops, so he was very self-satisfied watching the victorious searchers showing off the metal box. Then Captain Florian dialed a number.

A hundred miles away, sitting in the family room of his Brooklyn house, Frank Anselmo picked up the phone. He was watching New York 1, the twenty-four television news station.

"I'm watching already," Anselmo replied to Florian.

In the foreground, a reporter was talking breathlessly; in the background, half a dozen policemen in various uniforms were walking in and out of a small wooden cabin bathed in eery light.

". . . informed sources report that forty thousand dollars in cash was uncovered in a locked strongbox found hidden in the wood stove in this cabin, which is the summer home of the late Detective Santos. Detective Santos was killed in a suspicious Bushwick drug shootout, which also claimed the lives of organized crime mobster Tino Zapatti and an innocent child. The question on law enforcement's mind is what was Detective Santos doing with forty thousand dollars in secreted cash? This is Frank Gannon reporting for New York One, live from Ulster County."

Marybeth jammed her car to a curbside stop, jumped out, and headed straight for Elaine Santos' door. It was clear that both women were deeply distressed, as they wordlessly wandered into the living room and sat down in front of the ongoing TV news report about Eddie Santos.

"Can you believe this shit? Now they call the Carver incident the 'Santos Case'—and they're demanding a revived Knapp Commission investigation of police corruption. We never set foot in that dump after Eddie's father died; the place is full of hornets," Elaine went on, in need of sharing her grief.

"Yeah. Busy hornets," Marybeth replied tartly.

Elaine caught the drift, and asked, "What's happening to me, Marybeth?"

"A coverup? A diversionary tactic? Both?" Marybeth speculated, with certainty in her voice.

But that was only the big picture. Marybeth came from a long line of Irish cops, and she instinctively identified with Elaine Santos' private nightmare: police widows and orphans had only one consolation, that their husband and father died a hero's death, in the line of duty, protecting his family and others.

To rob Eddie Santos of his honor was to forever spiritually gut his wife and children. And if he were formally found to be a corrupt cop, they would also be materially impoverished through denial of his pension.

There was never any question that Marybeth Cogan would not become a Wall Street lawyer when she graduated Fordham Law School. Those firms didn't want "blue-collar" Catholic law school graduates any more than she wanted them. Marybeth Cogan was a cop's daughter, a cop's granddaughter, and a cop's great granddaughter. And Ms. Cogan only wanted to work with cops. Marybeth had an unusual sensibility to empathize with other people's suffering, and seeing Elaine's entrapment reinforced her commitment to the clergy in blue; and she was determined to help the Santos family.

The women sat despondently watching Deputy Mayor Calhoun conduct an ad hoc press conference on the steps of City Hall. He made a brief extemporaneous statement to the cameras and then stood for questions.

"The mayor understands the implications of the state troopers' discovery in Ulster County this morning, but he would like to stress these are implications only. Moreover, until a connection can be made between Detective Santos and the forty thousand dollars—or it can be determined from where this money was issued, no conclusions can be drawn," he offered as an opening comment. "Any questions?"

"Forty thousand dollars in a cop's strongbox, the guy had to be doing something wrong!" a radio reporter added half as a question and half in editorial comment.

"Detective Santos was a valued member of the department. Until the investigation is completed, we can assume nothing wrong has been done," Calhoun replied.

"How does a detective get forty thousand dollars?" a second reporter said accusingly.

"Perhaps he was thrifty," Calhoun answered ducking the question.

"What about the Zapatti connection? Was he dealing with Tino?" a print reporter shouted.

"Detective Santos was a veteran police officer. Part of his job was developing contacts with the underworld," he said trying to sound matter-of-fact.

"What about the strongbox? Doesn't it seem weird to you?" another reporter pressed him.

"Nothing seems weird until we have the facts," Kevin concluded.

Elaine rose robotically to answer her ringing phone.

A man's scratchy voice, desperate-sounding

said, "There's only two people in this world who know that's not Eddie's money they found. *You.*" A pause, *"And me."*

"Who is this?" Elaine demanded. She snapped her fingers to get Marybeth's attention, then pointed to the receiver and to the staircase to her bedroom. Marybeth ran upstairs, very carefully lifted the receiver off the hook and listened in.

"You have to tell me who this is," Elaine was insisting. "Otherwise how do I know you're not some pervert pulling a prank?"

"You're wasting time," the voice said roughly. "Never mind who I am. All you need to know right now is I'm the person who's willing to get you out of this. I can deliver the pension and the medals and everything you and your kids got coming to you. You want 'em?" he said, urging her to join him.

"But who are you?" she asked again.

"You want 'em or don't you?" the voice replied gruffly.

"Sure. I want them. Most of all, I want Eddie's name cleared," she replied firmly.

"I hear you," the voice said, suddenly softening. "I want to help you, but you got to help me, too."

"What does that mean?" Elaine inquired.

"I want to get the fuck out of this city. I'm

going to get clipped if I hang around here anymore."

"We gotta get outta here!" Cookie said desperately in the background.

"What do you need?" Elaine asked.

"Two airplane tickets to someplace warm. We'll tell you where. And ten thousand dollars in cash," Vinnie spat out in pain.

"Ten thousand dollars, for God's sake I can't—" she cried, before being interrupted by Marybeth.

"We're talking a lot of money. What have you got?" Marybeth asked indecisively.

"Who the hell are you?" he demanded in fear. And in the background Cookie could be heard pulling on his shoulder with a repeated "What's happening?"

"Marybeth Cogan, Detective Endowment Association. I'm the family's lawyer, assigned to protect Eddie's pension. I'm not a cop." And she demanded again, "What have you got?"

"I'm the goomba who set up the meeting for Eddie with Tino, so he could give up what he knew about the judge."

"And what was that?" Marybeth persisted. "Did someone bribe the judge?"

"I ain't saying no more. I gotta be sure I'll have someplace to go after I tell you," Vinnie responded with growing dejection.

"We're dead if we don't get out of here soon, Cookie added from behind him.

"Ten thousand and the plane tickets. Yes or no?" Vinnie was about to hang up. "I'll give you the destination later."

"Your information is worth nothing, unless I can bring a witness."

"A who?"

"A witness."

"You're disturbed."

"Then no deal."

"No cops!"

"No cops."

"I gave you a taste, because I know you need me," Vinnie said half-heartedly. "So don't screw up. I'll be watching you."

"You need me just as badly. Now where do we meet?" Marybeth said conclusively. And Vinnie compliantly gave her the destination.

Marybeth had an uncommon practicality, which kept her from going up blind alleys. While she felt uncomfortable with the deputy mayor's big-picture orientation toward politics and power, in contrast with her focus on doing some tangible good things for a single individual, she knew that he was honest and the most available credible witness she could get for her meeting with Vinnie.

After a difficult day in the bowels of government bureaucracy, Marybeth and Kevin gained a sense of renewal from the vibrancy of their surroundings, as they drove together up the East River Drive to their meeting with Vinnie Zapatti at Spuyten Divil, the turbulent crosscurrent at the intersection of the Hudson and East Rivers.

The Brooklyn and Williamsburg bridges spanned the East River like a double strand of natural pearls twinkling energetically on a beautiful black neck. Fulton Landing sparkled its reminiscences of a once sublime Brooklyn. Pepsico's signage blinked its unmistakable message in red from Queens, that brand-name consumer products were king today, while the United Nations nodded back with a reminder from its glass-and-stone headquarters on the Manhattan side that its message of peace was harder but more important to communicate to a world preoccupied with consumerism.

"A cop, a punk, a child, a perfect judge, and a bunch of Zapattis—that's a lot to take in. Which Zapatti are we meeting?" Calhoun inquired as they drove north.

"Big Paulie had two brothers, Tino was John's boy, Vinnie is Jimmy's."

"Why did you bother to bring me?" Calhoun asked, finally getting to the question that was really on his mind during all of the small talk.

"Because you're the most important person I know in city government. And if Vinnie Zapatti is willing to talk in front of you, my client's home free," Marybeth replied earnestly.

Calhoun gave a skeptical sigh, indicating that he was not impressed by Santos' prospects.

Marybeth interpreted his sigh as an arrogant distancing of himself from such insignificant matters as Eddie Santos' family's survival. And she lashed out at Calhoun.

"If you're such a big shot, then why don't you run for office instead of carrying the mayor's bag?"

"I consider it an honor not only to carry his bag but also to fill it at night with the things I think the city needs," Calhoun answered with the self-assuredness of a master accompanist to a great virtuoso.

"The kingmaker, the man behind the throne," Marybeth said mockingly.

"You don't like politicians?" Kevin asked evenly.

"You're no politician. Politicians run for office. You're a walker," Marybeth shot back derisively.

"My father used to say lawyers are like teenagers. You can't do anything about either of them. But y'know what?" Kevin added disarmingly.

"What?"

"Sometimes teenagers can be sexy as hell."

Marybeth was silent in response to what was supposed to be a backhanded compliment, because for a rare moment she genuinely didn't know what to say.

Sutton Place's opulent river-view apartments told who paid the taxes in New York, but soon melted into the dilapidated housing which lined the Harlem River Drive. Finally, they pulled to a stop at the rotting, deserted Spuyten Divil piers.

"Where are we? Calhoun asked, taking the conversation back to the business at hand.

"Dyckman Street. The northern tip of Manhattan. Drugtown Central, New York City. If Peter Stuyvesant had been smart he would've franchised these corners before the Dominicans got control of them and did it," Marybeth said with a twinkle.

"Vinnie sure likes spooky places. It looks like Monday night in Key Largo," Calhoun suggested, making reference to his favorite Bogart film.

"Vinnie's impersonating Mafia. He's a joke to his uncle. But a dangerous joke. As far as I'm concerned, they're all dangerous jokes," she said disparagingly.

"I wouldn't write these folks off yet," Calhoun offered cautiously.

"I said they were dangerous," Marybeth spat out, somewhat annoyed at his condescending tone.

A chilling wind whipped across the seemingly lifeless docks, but Marybeth and Calhoun soon realized that they were not alone. Frenzied squeaking, squealing, and scratching from hundreds of red- and purple-eyed wharf rats the size of well-fed small dogs created a frightening din as they savagely ripped apart collapsing garbage bags that restaurant owners had illegally dumped on the piers to avoid carting and disposal fees. Marybeth warned Kevin to stay far away from *ratus ratus*, as the hardy New York variety was scientifically labeled to distinguish it from its milder European cousin *ratus Norvegicus*, because if cornered *ratus ratus* could spring off its hind legs and rip out a human's throat.

Pathetic stinkpots lay moored in their grungy slips, half of them rotten and empty. Calhoun and Marybeth walked hastily to the end of one of them which sported a sign "112."

"What is this? Is this the place?" Marybeth asked with growing anxiety in her voice.

"This is the place. And it's the wrong place . . . And this is an invitation I should have declined," Calhoun replied nervously.

"C'mon," Marybeth urged both of them on.

"Nada," she concluded after searching for a couple of minutes.

"Do you think Vinnie had a change of heart? Calhoun wondered aloud.

"If he's a Zapatti, he has no heart," Marybeth said with disgust dripping from her words.

"Let's get out of here," Calhoun suggested, starting to turn Marybeth around toward the car.

"Don't turn around," Vinnie commanded in a harsh voice. He rubbed his aching sleepless red eyes, as they peered menacingly from their engulfing blackness.

Marybeth and Calhoun froze. And Marybeth wished now that she had prayed harder in Catholic school.

If youth was defined by curiosity, physical well being, and optimism then Vinnie was constructively eighty-five years old rather than his chronological twenty-one years; he was bathed in brutish ignorance, physically depleted by drug and alcohol abuse, and trembling legitimately in fear for his life.

"Who is this?" Vennie demanded from Marybeth.

"The deputy mayor."

"The deputy mayor? What do I need you

for?" Vinnie asked sarcastically, poking a snub nosed revolver in his back.

Although Vinnie held the gun, a quivering hand and voice betrayed his submissiveness to the victims—unless he panicked or the gun went off by accident.

"Don't get smart, Vinnie. I'm the only prayer you've got," Marybeth said challengingly.

Vinnie stood behind them and patted Calhoun down for weapons.

"Let's go," he ordered abruptly.

"I thought you said slip one-twelve?" Marybeth protested for no reason at all.

"I did, that's how I got a preview of you. It's one-nineteen," Vinnie said with evident satisfaction at his own cleverness. "Move!" A comfort zone seemed to have emerged among the group, so they could now conduct business with a modicum of order.

A few minutes later, the unlikely trio were sailing down the coast of Manhattan island. Vinnie Zapatti proudly manned the tiller of his dilapidated old inboard, its deck shiny-wet from a pinhead leak. Calhoun and Marybeth sat huddled next to each other, shivering from the cold, and keeping an uneasy eye on the shoreline rushing past. As the unworthy vessel was buffeted by the tricky currents that converged in the Spuyten Divil, they looked up at

the heavy, graceless iron trackwork of the huge
railroad bridge towering overhead, in order to
avoid getting sick. They both heaved sighs of
relief when they finally entered the calmer
reaches of the Hudson River.

"This is a SeaRider?" Calhoun asked, trying
to make sure that Vinnie didn't totally zone
out.

"You probably sailed SeaRiders at your
country club," Vinnie suggested jealously.
"This is no fucking SeaRider. This is a piece of
shit they call a SurfRider. I wanted the Sea-
Rider but my uncle wouldn't pop for it."

"Does your uncle like boats?" Marybeth
asked inanely. Calhoun shot her a glance, but
she shrugged her shoulders as if to say "Give
me a break, I'm nervous."

"My uncle wouldn't know a cleaver from a
cleat," Vinnie said flatly. "It's my dream, you
know, to run a charter down in the islands."

Calhoun found it reassuring that Vinnie
steered expertly past several buoys. Maybe
there was some remote element of reality behind this crazy fantasy after all. And, more
immediately, maybe Vinnie wouldn't end up
drowning them all.

"That's Fort Lee, New Jersey over there,"
Vinnie said pointing to the farther shore.
"They buried Tino there, only a few feet from
where Aaron Burr offed Alexander Hamilton."

Calhoun shot a glance at Marybeth, communicating his thought that this was becoming too surreal, being adrift in the middle of the Hudson River with a homicidal maniac giving a history lesson.

"What is going on?" Vinnie shouted suspiciously.

"We're thinking that you must be a history buff," Marybeth said cautiously.

"Yeah," Vinnie admitted modestly. "I know each inch of this river and both shores. Aaron Burr wanted more land south of the Texas border, but Hamilton wouldn't go for it, so he took him out. I'd like to sail around Nevis. That's the island where Hamilton was born. Bet you didn't know that."

"You're right there, Vinnie," Calhoun admitted.

"Bet you didn't know Hamilton was a fruit, either," Vinnie said proudly.

"You're just full of surprises, aren't you?" Calhoun acknowledged.

"I might even be in Nevis now if only crazy Eddie didn't bag me on my last coke run. And even then, I'd be home free if Tino hadn't gotten the drop on Eddie," Vinnie said plaintively. "I had it all worked out. None of this was supposed to happen. All Eddie wanted was information on the judge."

"How do you know that?" Calhoun asked.

"Because I was there that morning," Vinnie replied.

"So you set him up? Calhoun continued.

"Hey, fuck you," Vinnie screamed. "No way I set him up."

"You knew Tino was looking at ten to twenty."

"Wrong, asshole!" Vinnie said. "Eddie wasn't there to take Tino down. He only wanted information on the judge."

"What information was that," Marybeth asked.

Vinnie's primitive eyes swung the door shut. "That you only get with ten thousand and the plane tickets," he said. "Come up with it by tomorrow. Our little meeting is adjourned."

Calhoun and Marybeth looked around nervously, and they both swallowed hard. After enjoying their moment of panic, Vinnie gunned the engine and turned the boat a hard left, returning to the battered pier overhanging the Manhattan shore.

"Let us bring you in, Vinnie," Calhoun ventured as Vinnie steaded the boat for them to disembark.

"We'll talk to the Feds and get you into the witness protection program," Marybeth added.

"I've got my own witness protection plan,"

Vinnie said adamantly. "What you need to do is fund it for me."

"We'll do our best," Marybeth replied evenly.

"I want the money and the tickets by tomorrow. I haven't got time for you to jerk me around. You save me, and I'll save Eddie's family, Miss Cogan. Counselor, I'll call you at your office at noon tomorrow so we can arrange the final meeting."

Thirty seconds later Vinnie was swallowed by the Hudson River darkness. Only the lapping water from a tiny wake against the rotting pilings indicated a boat had ever been there.

The next morning Cookie waited near a phone booth in Sheepshead Bay for the planned all-clear call from Vinnie, which would then trigger a meeting at his apartment to pack for their long-awaited escape south.

The radio in her green Camaro blasted Tina Turner's "Private Dancer," while Cookie sang along with her whole body shimmying voluptuously on the curbside. Cookie turned up the music and snapped her fingers even harder as her anxiety grew with Vinnie's failure to call.

A car drove by and Cookie instinctively looked over her shoulder, nervously trying to catch a glimpse of its occupants as it disappeared. A second car moved slowly down the street, its passengers seeming to rubber-neck at the Sheepshead Bay fishing fleet bobbing in the background. The vehicle approached the phone booth and practically slowed to a stop.

A rear-seated gunman, Eddie "The Sandman" Strafaci, lowered his window and blasted away at point-blank range, pow, pow, pow, into Cookie's pretty head; he was still firing as Cookie careened lifeless off the shattered glass telephone booth.

Also at dawn, deckhand Ken Tuminski leaned over the side of the tug to pee into the Hudson River. Ken's tinkling stopped when he spotted a small unmanned craft drifting toward the tug. He alerted Captain Smith to steer abreast of the boat, which appeared to have a heavy drag at its stern. Extending the long gaff of his docking pole behind the stern, Tuminski pulled Vinnie Zapatti's bloated body to the surface, firmly wrapped at the hands, waist, and legs with the SurfRider's anchor chain. Captain Smith ordered his deckhand to hold the derelict craft in place, while he notified the police.

It was unusual for the mayor's secretary to call Calhoun so early in the morning at home and order him to come directly to the mayor's office without offering any explanation. By

7:30 AM he hurried up the back staircase from the basement entrance to City Hall, sensing that something was happening by observing the milling horde of reporters and police brass on the front steps.

In his dash past the Intel desk guarding access to the mayor's wing, Calhoun forgot to acknowledge Bobby, but Bobby did not forget about Kevin. "Good morning, Kevin," he said with an accompanying cough.

"Good morning, Bobby," Kevin replied, stopping in his tracks to absorb the vibrations of an alert.

Kevin noticed Bobby's eyes shift toward the police operations fax, which churned out bulletins, reports, and orders, just as Police Commissioner Coonan and Captain Florian emerged from the mayor's office. They nodded a businesslike hello to Kevin and quickly moved by him. Calhoun leaned over the fax to read:

"Vincent Zapatti, fished out of the Hudson River near the 79th Street Boat Basin. Hands and feet were bound in a three-inch anchor chain, ship's chandlery-type. Preliminary forensics reveal torture and drowning after a blow to the head from a blunt instrument." Kevin ripped off the entire report and kept reading the details, including those about Cookie's murder.

"Another Zapatti; the sharks are already circling," Bobby observed, pointing to the press filing into the Blue Room for a conference.

Abe rushed by on his way to the press conference and muttered to Kevin and Bobby, "You know what the Talmud says, don't you? 'Shrouds have no pockets.'"

Calhoun raised his eyebrows.

"You want better, I'll give better," Abe offered. "'Dead men tell no tales.'"

Kevin knocked on the mayor's door and entered. Mayor Pappas stood with his back to the door, staring reflectively out of the floor-to-ceiling window into City Hall Park. He did not turn around for a full minute. Kevin uncomfortably allowed his eyes to wander up and down the glazed walls of the high-ceilinged Victorian office. Its antiques and early American paintings, loaned to each mayor by the Metropolitan Museum of Art, and the stuffed chintz hand-me-down furniture with a large nineteenth century desk at its center in front of the marble fireplace, conveyed a comfortable, more personal lifestyle of a bygone era. However, three open tabloids on the mayor's desk, flashing telephone lights, and secretarial buzzes served as reminders that these were anything but stable times for the mayor.

"Where you been?" the mayor finally asked, without turning around.

"Busy night," Calhoun answered evasively.

"Yeah?" was all the mayor said, urging Kevin to come clean before being confronted.

"You saw this morning's operations print-outs?" Calhoun asked, knowing the answer.

"What about it?" The mayor started to pace the perimeter of his office, fingering a long, thick unlit cigar.

"I was with Vinnie Zapatti last night," Kevin confessed.

The mayor turned around abruptly and focused his eyes intently on his deputy.

"He's dead because of Tino Zapatti's probation report," Calhoun continued. "Five deaths and they're connected, that's all I know. That I learned from Vinnie." Kevin sounded excited from the chase and ready for more.

"And that's all I want to know," Mayor Pappas protested with a steely look, reflecting his conviction from long experience that a politician should never draw a curtain back, unless he knew exactly what was behind it.

"I'm just trying to circle the wagons . . ." Calhoun responded defensively.

"You're trying to help me? Who do you think you are, some gumshoe in a dime novel? Loose-cannoning around the city, consorting with known mobsters. You're my right hand.

You're the mayor's right hand. What are you fucking around for?" the mayor said raising his voice with genuine alarm. He tried to get Calhoun to understand that he was an exposed public official, not an isolated private person who could pursue his curiosity without concern for appearance and impact.

The mayor shut his eyes, thinking. Then he opened them and spoke softly, pointing to the portrait of LaGuardia that hung behind his desk.

"My desk was used by Fiorello LaGuardia, the Little Flower. He was five foot tall, read the funny papers on the radio to his constituents' children, and was the best goddamn mayor this city ever had. You know what La-Guardia said? 'Why is it that every time you can do some good, the "nice people" come in and mess you up?'" After hesitating a moment, he added, "Be nice Kevin, but don't mess me up. Men are destroyed more often by their friends, than by their enemies."

"I hear you, sir," Kevin said rigidly, hurrying out the door, while avoiding the mayor's eyes.

The mayor had never spoken to his shocked deputy that way before. Kevin recalled his mother admonishing his father: "Life is a symphony and you keep playing one note." He wondered whether he was missing the bigger picture by being so obsessed with the possibility of judicial corruption that he believed struck at the very heart of political democracy.

Calhoun rushed to his offices, slammed the door behind him and dialed the phone.

"Hello?" answered Marybeth.

"I woke you up," Calhoun said apologetically.

"Are you crazy? I've been up half the night trying to figure out how to raise ten thousand dollars. The hook is in. I'm close. Vinnie is Eddie Santos' passport to an honorable death. All I've got to do is reel him in now," she reported full of hope.

"Vinnie's dead," Calhoun deadpanned.

"What?" Kevin could hear Marybeth's stunned reaction.

"Vinnie Zapatti. He surfaced in the Seventy-ninth Street Boat Basin this morning. His girlfriend was executed in Sheepshead Bay," Kevin followed up grimly.

Marybeth and Kevin both fell silent in contemplation of these large events, until she said, "Keep talking, Kevin."

"If Vinnie's foot hadn't gotten caught in the doughnut," Kevin said stumbling along.

"In the what?" she asked in puzzlement.

"The life preserver, he would've floated right out under the Verrazano Bridge and back to his forebears in Sicily," Calhoun said with some fright at his own observation.

"Oh God!"

"Heads up," he warned Marybeth.

"For what?"

"We don't know yet. But we were the last ones to see Vinnie, and his murderers don't know how much he told us," Kevin said with the hairs standing up on his arms.

"You're beginning to sound like Holly," she responded with deepening fear.

"He's beginning to make sense." Kevin knew that since awful things had already happened, more bad things were going to happen.

There was a pregnant pause, and Calhoun felt Marybeth had something she wanted to say.

"What?" he asked.

"Poor Vinnie," was her sad response. "What are you going to do?"

"Whatever I have to," the deputy mayor replied with clear-eyed iron determination.

CHAPTER NINETEEN

Calhoun asked the desk sergeant at the Fifty-first Precinct for directions to the homicide detectives squad room. The cop pointed to a little door on his right, without ever looking up from the *Sports Illustrated* in front of him.

The deputy mayor did not knock before entering the squad room. Inside four detectives sat around a circular wooden table covered with stained manila homicide case folders, *Playboy*, *The New York Post* and *The Daily Enquirer*. Behind them was a large white cardboard tacked to the wall, with a description of each precinct homicide penciled in; a case successfully closed had a giant red X marked through the rectangular box containing that homicide.

As the detectives continued to drink coffee and smoke, Holly rose from their midst.

"I'll see you later," he told them and all three quickly disappeared.

"I don't have a lot of time today," Holly continued, confronting Calhoun.

"I cleared this with Captain Gillardi. He said for you to take all the time you need."

"You pulling rank on me?" Holly became infuriated.

"Yes."

"Looking for a new shoe size?" Holly yelled, nose-to-nose with Calhoun.

"Cement-C," Kevin said without backing off. "I know the joke, Holly. What I need now are the straight lines."

Holly stared at him belligerently, as Calhoun continued: "Okay, I'm going to give it to you bad. The police commissioner works for the mayor."

"What's your point?" a defeated Holly asked.

"Trust me or fuck you," Calhoun said with perfect clarity.

"Stand up! I want to see how many people I'm talking to."

And with that order, Holly placed his hands in Calhoun's armpits and yanked him up from his chair in a single motion. Holly methodically patted him down for a wire. When Calhoun proved to be clean, Holly's mood changed. The hostility was gone, and only anxiety remained. They sat down knee to knee for their discussion.

"Eddie called me from Manhattan South," Holly started.

"The night before?"

"Yeah, he wanted me to come with him," Holly recalled looking off into space.

Calhoun studied Holly and recognized his self-loathing at having failed his partner.

"You didn't go. You did the right thing," Kevin volunteered with genuine compassion.

"No, I didn't. He had no business going up there without a ghost. That should have been me. Plus a raft of backups." Holly stopped, reliving his nightmare. Then he said, "But Eddie was such a hothead . . . the kind that never cools off; he was not willing to let go."

"Of what? What did Eddie find out?" Calhoun insisted relentlessly.

"There was another probation report. It set Tino up for the max—ten to twenty," Holly stuttered, intuitively knowing the consequences of his words.

"What happened to it?" Calhoun asked with surprise.

"I don't know."

"Who wrote it?" Calhoun pressured Holly for an answer.

"That's all I got," Holly uttered quietly.

Holly's eyes were wet, as he went on talking largely to himself. "I've got this old boat. But I'm going to sell it. I'm going to give the money to Eddie's kids."

Calhoun considered this broken man who had nothing more to give.

"You keep that boat, Holly, that boat is good for you," he said softly.

As Calhoun headed for the door, Holly called out.

"Mr. Calhoun!"

"Yeah?"

"The probation officer. . . ." He started to speak but panicked.

"Name?" Calhoun said encouragingly.

"James Wakely." Holly said, his words nailing down the key identification. "But you won't find him on Leonard Street."

"Where is he?" Calhoun demanded.

"Upstate. Working parole," Holly replied, his shoulders crumbling from the stress and his unfixable regrets.

Elaine's feelings of helplessness flowed over their banks. She was compelled to do something to vent her rage and anguish.

Without warning, except for a well-placed tip to City Hall's Room Nine press corps, a veiled Mrs. Santos appeared on the steps of Brooklyn County Courthouse next to Mr. Bone, dressed in widow's black. Avoiding ceremonial gestures she pinned Eddie's gold detective shield, touching his own silver star from Vietnam, on Bone's chest.

"Eddie would want you to have this," Elaine said simply. "We're little people," she said, tears streaming down her cheeks; pausing she leaned on Bone for support, then from this position she continued looking straight into the TV cameras. "We're both victims of the big guys' politics, corruption, and coverup."

Caught by surprise, the photographers begged Elaine to repin Bone; they assured her that this would be the front page picture on every newspaper. Mrs. Santos went through the pinning again with equivalent drama, crossed herself for the nightly news, and vanished as quickly as she had appeared.

There was a sullen and threatening quality to the weathered stones of the walls and towers of Attica which rose aggressively from the soft green countryside surrounding the prison. After unwelcome national prominence during riots in the late 1970s, the prison had lumbered back into obscurity. Once the media had gone, the guards quietly, and sometimes brutally, settled scores with the prisoners. At the same time, the authorities began making structural changes, instituting regulations and procedures aimed at making sure that another uprising never would or ever could take place. Anger and frustration seeped into Attica's walls and turned the place mean and bitter, as thousands of men in successive generations were forced to swallow their pride and their rage.

The Attica system did not welcome spur-of-the-moment visitors; and it welcomed VIP visitors even less. The Deputy Mayor of the City of New York and the Counsel of the Detective's Endowment Association, therefore, had to wait almost an hour in a sparsely furnished reception room before a deputy warden was able to come down and size them up. It made no difference that they wanted to see a member of the staff rather than a prisoner; outsiders generally meant trouble no matter whom they wished to see. It took the deputy warden almost another hour to locate the employee and to arrange a meeting. Finally a guard arrived and escorted them through a series of long corridors with double-lock doors at each end. The first two were opened by the guard's keys; the next two were electronically controlled and only opened based on visual recognition by guards watching through windows of bulletproof glass.

They finally reached a large and freshly painted metal door with a keypad set in the wall next to it. The guard punched in five numbers and a loud click echoed back from the concrete floor. The guard opened the door and gestured Kevin and Marybeth to enter. They entered a large room dominated by a highly polished wooden table surrounded by half a dozen leather-seated wooden chairs. A thick, dark-green carpet covered the floor from wall to wall. The far end of the room was turned into a mini-shrine by an American flag in one corner and a New York State flag in the other. On the wall between them were large framed photographs of the president and the governor.

The young guard spoke to them for the first time. "This is the VIP visitor's room," he said with a touch of awe in his voice. "It doesn't get used very often," he added apologetically, as he ran his finger through the layer of dust that covered the table. "Have a seat," he said, "Mr. Wakely should be here soon."

Kevin and Marybeth sat together at the big table. The teeming noise of prison life, raging beyond this incongruous room, was completely muted. Only the groaning of the prison's massive furnaces and the clanking of the miles of pipes managed to sneak through the silence. Suddenly the door at the far end of the room swung open and a short, carelessly dressed man limped through it.

"I told you people not to come up here," he said angrily as he moved towards them. He ignored Calhoun's outstretched hand. "You've made a long trip for nothing," he continued.

Marybeth regarded him coldly. "For your sake, I hope that isn't true, Mr. Wakely," she said. Because you can tell us the truth now, or you can tell it under oath on the witness stand."

Wakely's eyebrows arched upwards and he shot a glance toward Calhoun. "You looking to grow a pair of brass balls, miss?" he sneered.

"No thank you," Marybeth snapped. "I'm doing well enough without them. Now, do you want a subpoena or may we continue?"

Wakely stood still for a moment and then took a seat on the other side of the table. He didn't say anything, but the set of his shoulders indicated that he had lost his bravado.

"What brought you up here, Mr. Wakely?" Calhoun asked gently.

Wakely seized the lifeline and answered Calhoun. "The job, of course. New York State Parole Officer. Better pay, better pension," he said with sing-song sarcasm.

"Nicer surroundings," Marybeth suggested.

Wakely either missed or decided to ignore the irony in her voice. "You think so?" he asked her with a crooked smile.

"What happened to Tino Zapatti?" Calhoun inquired bluntly.

"He's dead, isn't he?"

"I'm talking about two years ago," the deputy mayor said sternly.

The parole officer sighed and began flexing his folded fingers.

"You might say that he got probation, but I ended up serving his sentence," Wakely said with a mirthless laugh. Wakely's demeanor grew deadly serious, and he continued, "When I squawked about the probation, Schwartzie made it clear that if I didn't leave the department I'd be labeled a chronic malcontent, and they'd terminate me. I was shocked. And I was pissed. I was young, and I was idealistic, and I wasn't going to be threatened. I told him to stuff it, that I was going to go public with my original report. And then I got a visit from a guy."

"Who was that?" Marybeth asked, missing Wakely's ominous tone.

"Just a wiseguy, miss, he didn't bother to tell me his name. But he showed up in my office on the sixth floor at Leonard Street. He was very thoughtful," Wakely said with twisted irony. "He said he could show me a better way than the elevator out of my office, and he threw a believable glance out of my window to underscore the point. So I decided that maybe I should reconsider my position. Schwartzie helped me get this job, and here my office is on the ground floor," Wakely finished with bitter resignation at the system that had victimized him.

"What sentence did you recommend?" Calhoun asked.

"Ten to twenty," Wakely replied. "There wasn't any choice if you read the rap sheet. Zapatti was picked up pushing drugs to kids in a school yard. Not even doing it himself; he got kids to deal for him. And it's hard to believe, but he also had a loaded weapon in his car, from a previous shooting. All that got lost in the second report."

"The *second* report?" Marybeth repeated.

"You mean you didn't write the good report the judge used?" Calhoun asked.

"More like the too-good-to-be-true report?" Wakely said contemptuously. "When I saw it, I almost fell over."

"Who wrote it?" Calhoun demanded. "Who ordered it?"

"That I don't know," Wakely answered.

"You didn't ask?" Marybeth said skeptically.

"No, I didn't ask," Wakely replied. "When I

felt the urge to move to the country, I forgot all about asking. I was too busy packing up my sixth-floor office before I got help from my earlier visitor."

"You must have suspicions," Marybeth pressed.

"Miss, I have a family, and I have a pension plan, and I have chronic acute lumbago. One thing I don't have is suspicions. Now, if you'll excuse me, you people better get out of here. My lumbago tells me snow is coming. You better hurry. Attica gets socked in pretty fast, and no one should spend any more time here than he absolutely has to."

Without shaking hands or saying good-bye, Wakely abruptly pushed back his chair and limped out with his hand against his aching back. Wakely penetrated successive gates and heavy metal doors, which locked noisily behind him. Shortly, the young guard returned to lead Kevin and Marybeth back to freedom.

Wakely's lumbago indeed proved to be a reliable weather forecaster. The Amtrak passenger train Marybeth and Kevin boarded in Buffalo inched its way through a blinding snowstorm, until it came to a full stop at a tiny station in Floyd, New York. Passengers could remain on board or traverse two hundred yards along a narrow path to the warmly lit Floyd Diner. A middle-aged, portly conductor set his lantern beside the train's steps and answered questions or offered assistance to passengers.

"How long?" Calhoun inquired.

"About an hour, but no telling," the conductor advised with the stoicism that comes from frequently experiencing forces greater than oneself.

"An hour?" Marybeth chimed in with impatient disbelief at their rotten luck.

"You don't want to suffocate in a tunnel, do you? They got to dig one out a few miles ahead; meanwhile, enjoy the snow," the conductor suggested, offering that gentle resignation was the best response to mother nature.

"I'm hungry. You can't eat snow," Calhoun finally said with an accepting wink.

"Try the diner over there."

"Any good?" asked Marybeth.

"It was last week when we got snowed in," the conductor said with a knowledgeable smile.

At the diner, a friendly waitress, used to dealing calmly with delayed passengers in distress took their order.

"I'll take a hamburger, french fries, and a Coke," Marybeth indicated, while looking at the menu.

"I'll have the lemon pudding. Everything to go, please," ordered Calhoun.

"You got it," the waitress said with a dazzling smile.

"These people are so relaxed. Maybe there is something to small-town life," Marybeth said with a bit of self-mockery about their own intensity.

"My dad is an archaeologist and spends a lot of time at digs in the middle of nowhere. Used to say he'd rather wake up beside the road in a sleeping bag than in any city in the world. There *is* something about solitude, being in touch with yourself. You ever wonder what we are doing hustling in New York?" Kevin asked half reflectively.

"We can make an impact on people's lives in New York. We certainly made a difference to Eddie Santos and his family. Now that we found Wakely, we can clear his name and get them their pension," Marybeth said with satisfaction.

"Whoa. Not so fast. We gotta keep Wakely on ice until we get our hands on that report," Calhoun replied giving his first indication that he had a broader agenda than helping the Santos family.

"We don't need the report. All we need are Holly's and Wakely's depositions," Marybeth insisted.

"That's all *you* need." Calhoun said, possessed with a purpose. "I gotta get my hands on that report, see what's in it, where it leads. We take Wakely's deposition now, and a number of interested parties might start working their shredding machines overtime."

"And how long is this gonna take? Three months? Six months? A year?" she demanded.

"It'll take what it takes. John Pappas is on the road to the White House, and it is my job to make sure there are no bumps on the road," he replied.

Marybeth studied his face, as if tracing something vulgar. She couldn't comprehend how ambition could override his feelings for a family in deep trouble.

"How noble of you. And while you're propping up your man, how's Elaine Santos supposed to feed and clothe her children?" Marybeth raised her voice for the first time. Their eyes met for a pregnant moment, when they confronted the reality of directly conflicting life orientations: she was focused on helping one person now and he was obsessed with systemic cleansing, somehow to more closely align ethics with daily behavior.

"I'm sorry about that. I really am," he said softly, but without any retreat.

"Yeah, I'm sure you are. And what if, while you're playing detective, James Wakely decides it might be healthier to disappear? We're left with nothing," Marybeth said, angry that he was willing to play Russian roulette with Elaine Santos' life.

"Suppose next month there's another Elaine Santos and then the month after that another? And month after month police widows and their kids banging on coffins, longing for their husbands and fathers and where are they? Gone. Why? We don't know because we were too scared to get to the bottom of this. Losing Eddie Santos' pension is a risk we have to take—if we're going to dig out the truth! This didn't just happen. We're on to something big. Schwartz wouldn't have acted without protective cover; maybe Anselmo was the engineer," Calhoun suggested with a combination of relish and excitement.

"I don't need you to get Wakely's deposition," she said falling back on client obligation. Then she continued more philosophically. "Your mind's fucked up with Anselmo beating you on BancExchange. Bosses exist because politicians need someone else to slaughter the cow so they can eat steak. Kevin, there is genius in knowing when to let go. Your demons are driving you into quicksand," Marybeth argued.

"Look, just because there were two reports, that still doesn't explain the forty thousand dollars. Now I don't think Eddie Santos is crooked, but you talk to Wakely on your own, and I guarantee you will feel the full weight of the mayor's office bearing down on you. And that is not a very pleasant feeling," Calhoun answered.

"You're a mean prick, you know that?"

"At City Hall, that's a compliment," he said, with a wiseguy grin.

Marybeth had enough of Calhoun's monstrous inhumanity and rudeness. As she stood up to leave, Kevin snapped back to reality, and he sincerely urged Marybeth to stay.

"Hold on a minute."

"To what? Your ambition? John Pappas' coattails?" she shouted.

"Burger, fries, Coke, and one lemon pudding," the waitress announced.

"I'll take this bag. Mayor's boy gets the one with the lemon pudding."

Marybeth grabbed the food and marched out into the snow as Calhoun peered through the window, watching her beat a path to the train as the waitress placed the other order in his hand.

Calhoun opened the Styrofoam take-out box and started to dig in. Suddenly he stood up and crossed to a pay phone, placing a buck slip from Abe on top of the phone. Calhoun's eyes examined the scribbling on it, "Lawrence Schwartz, Probation Dept., Branch Officer," along with an office and home phone number. And he dialed decisively.

"Hello?" Schwartz answered with tentative retreat in his voice.

"Mr. Schwartz? Kevin Calhoun. I've just been talking to a friend of yours, a Mr. Wakely."

The train whistle sounded a loud warning blast to reboard; Kevin finished his conversation with Schwartz quickly and rushed out of the Floyd Diner.

Mayor Pappas hated the politically claustrophobic feeling of being besieged, dealing with crises instead of creating positive change, so he particularly welcomed the opportunity to address young people at Columbia University's special convocation in honor of its newly appointed president. The blazing lights of the Columbia campus reflected a mysteriously inviting glow through the wall of snow being driven by high winds across its open lawns.

Mayor Pappas jumped out of his limo, which parked on the cobblestone path at the campus center, and bounded through the snowstorm, ahead of his bodyguards, and up the steep stone steps into the huge rotunda of Low Memorial Library. A thousand eager young students applauded the mayor, as they searched for a character insight into his success, which they might imitate. President Ruff led him to the podium and admiringly witnessed the mayor virtually sucking in the positive energy from his highly receptive audience, moving forward, backward, and side to side on the platform, waving and smiling in every direction.

After appropriate greetings and recognitions, Mayor Pappas enthusiastically launched into the substance of his message.

"I stayed in public life in the hope of being joined in the struggle by others, who can help make change possible. Who are these others? You! Because by the time people reach my age, many of us have been too anesthetized by habit, materialism, family obligations, and fear to cope with the sacrifices of public service.

"I know that many of you are working hard for diplomas in business, medicine, law, and other fields which lead to financial reward. But you are too young to settle for a life which repeats itself for decades on end. Don't play at life, pretending to be happy in the fast lane, when in fact, life is passing *you* by. Youth is a time for restlessness, action, and struggle. Feeling alive makes life worth living, especially if the intensity comes from helping others.

"So I'm asking you to put aside materialism for the time being and join in the struggle, because the turbulent waters of public service are consistent with your present life force. Tennessee Williams explained it in a letter describing his thoughts at the time he was writing *A Streetcar Named Desire:*

" '. . . The heart of man, his body and his brain, are forged in a white-hot furnace for the purpose of conflict . . . and that with the conflict removed, the man is a sword cutting daisies . . . that not privation but luxury is the wolf at the door . . .'

"You can be the energy for politicians like me; the conscience who holds the mirror before our faces; the knowledge which brings possibility and a better tomorrow. I urge you all to join in a salute to struggle, a salute to life, a salute to the public man."

The young audience, joined by faculty on the platform, was on its feet giving the mayor a standing ovation. The mayor in turn was applauding the students. He seemed to be visibly recharged, newly committed, as he leaped from the stage to mingle freely with the students.

The deepening snow had turned wet and this necessitated that Judge and Mrs. Stern spend the night in their son's elegant suburban home. Nobody minded, because Judge Stern seemed to exhibit immeasurable joy and freedom playing with his grandchildren, momentarily forgetting his ordeal. Mrs. Stern looked out of the large picture window and was shocked to see a drenched, unflinching black man staring at the house from the sidewalk.

"Oh my God, *he's* there. Walter, make him leave us alone," she cried.

"Bone has no one left but us," Judge Stern whispered in response.

With this observation, Judge Stern took a large black umbrella and walked toward the door.

"Dad, let me go with you," his son begged.

"I must talk to him alone," Judge Stern replied with determination.

The Stern family looked on through the window in horror, as Walter Stern crossed the snow covered lawn under his umbrella. He confronted his accuser, a breathing corpse. Judge Stern parted his lips as if to speak, but no words came out. He handed Bone his umbrella and started his return to the house in silent contemplation, when Edgar Bone uttered his first words: "Good-bye, Your Honor," in a highly respectful tone.

Judge Stern abjectly opened the door to re-enter his son's house, a thoroughly defeated man who was on the verge of a nervous breakdown. His wife rushed to embrace him, crying, clinging desperately to her man.

"Did you explain things to him Walter," she prayed.

"My lips parted but no sound came out. What can I explain to this demolished soul? 'Mr. Bone, I didn't mean to bribe my way into becoming a judge,'" he said, coming to a full stop, as if in order to contemplate his own sin.

Then Judge Stern continued speaking, with self-loathing in his voice. "'It seemed all right at the time because everyone in the establishment knew that was the system and winked at it. But in daylight it looked very bad. I was blackmailed into fixing the Zapatti case . . . I let them convince me that my values didn't apply to the world I found myself in . . . because it was convenient to save my skin. I knew Tino was a vicious animal, but I didn't know he would kill *your* Robby. You can't expect consistency in an inconsistent world . . . it was a minor lapse, so please forgive me . . . We have to take the world as we find it . . .

don't we, Mr. Bone? Sorry you are a casualty.' "

Mrs. Stern became hysterical.

"Walter . . . stop it! What are you saying?" she screamed.

"Dad, what are we going to do?" his son asked more objectively from within his own state of shock.

"I can't sleep; I can't eat; I can't walk straight; I can't smile; I can't even enjoy my grandchildren in peace. There's only one thing to do . . . return to what I believe in . . . the law," he said with a soulful commitment.

His wife, son, and grandchildren enveloped Walter Stern in a totally loving embrace, knowing that this was a good man done in by a wicked system.

Larry Schwartz hastily walked away from his apartment building in Stuyvesant Town. As he worked his way through the snow on Avenue C, looking nervously in every direction but in front of him, Larry caught his foot in a snow-bank and slipped to the ground. A yellow-brown interoffice envelope flipped from his hand and Schwartz crawled through the snow on his belly to instantly retrieve it. Neglecting to brush himself off, Schwartz reestablished his pace until arriving at a pay phone on the wall in front of an all-night Korean grocer on Fourteenth and C. He proceeded about a hundred steps beyond the phone, pivoted 360 degrees with eyes darting madly, quickly returned to the phone, and dialed a number scribbled on his hand.

Kevin awoke to the ringing and answered sleepily. "Calhoun here."

"I got it! Meet me in back of the Korean's on Fourteenth and C," the voice babbled.

"Schwartz?" Calhoun asked.

"I got the fuckin' probation report. Take it out of my hands," he begged in a trembling voice.

A lone man in a long trenchcoat exited the passenger seat of the black town car, which idled curbside in front of the grocer. Schwartz heard the rustling of a brown paper bag in the man's hand next to him and turned with eyes as big as half dollars to witness the gunman pump a single bullet through the bag into his brain. The executioner yanked the probation report from his victim's tightly clasped grip and slowly returned to his car as Schwartz's blood dyed the fresh white snow dark red.

Calhoun pressed the receiver to his ear so hard it began to hurt. Straining to hear something—praying to hear *anything*—he waited until the seconds of silence had turned into minutes.

"Schwartz . . . Schwartz . . ." Kevin kept yelling the name into the receiver until the sound finally numbed some of the emotions flooding over him. Slowly, and almost tenderly, he placed the receiver on the table, as if this gentle treatment could somehow lessen the pain that Lawrence Schwartz might still be suffering. Kevin's racing mind subconsciously reviewed the situation and suddenly arrived at a stunning realization.

Reaching over he flipped off the wall switch, plunging the room into darkness. Clinging with his back to the wall of his Greenwich Village studio, Kevin slid to the window. Keeping in the shadow, he looked into the street below. A black town car had just double-parked across the street from the entrance of his building. The driver remained behind the wheel, while two tall, burly men, one wearing a long trenchhcoat and the other a dark-colored quilted parka with the hood pulled up exited the car and crossed the street toward his building. They moved like they knew exactly where they were going and what they wanted, swiftly and purposefully, without looking anywhere but straight ahead. Watching them, Kevin felt his skin begin to tingle.

Threading quickly through the familiar terrain of his darkened apartment, Kevin grabbed his coat and slipped quietly out into the hall. The illuminated numbers above the elevator indicated that the car was on its way up. Running down the remainder of the corridor, Kevin entered the fire stairs just as he heard the elevator doors begin to open.

Kevin felt a curiously controlled panic as he literally flung his body down the stairwell. Taking three steps at a time, Calhoun used the handrail like a vault pole, propelling himself ever faster in the direction gravity was already pulling him. Ten stories down, at the garage level, he cautiously opened the door into the underground parking area. The cavernous concrete space was brilliantly lit by overhead florescent tubes and was eerily quiet. Moving stealthily along the wall toward his parked vehicle, Kevin tensed when he saw that the elevator was at the sixth floor and heading downward. Looking quickly from side to side, he sprinted into the driver's seat.

Inserting the key in the ignition, he found himself hesitating to turn it. Instead he sat staring for a long second at his fingers on the silver oval, while explosive images of detonated car bombs from a hundred movies and TV shows flashed through his head. In the rear view mirror he saw the elevator door start to open and he saw two tall figures rushing through it. With no more time to spare, he started the ignition. The engine turned over and reacted immediately to the surge of fuel his foot was pumping into it. The car jumped forward with a screeching of rubber on concrete. Kevin thought he heard shouts behind him as he gunned the car up the circular ramp and out into the street.

The deputy mayor kept sneaking worried glances in the rear view mirror, breathing sighs of relief whenever there were no headlights behind him. Kevin's fingers hit RECALL 02 on his cellular phone. Abe's wife gave him the number where her husband could be reached and Calhoun gropingly dialed it. During a brief conversation describing the present circumstances, Kevin maneuvered into the lane leading to the Brooklyn Bridge's on-ramp.

The brightly lit bustling interior of The Famous, Brooklyn's legendary deli on Thirteenth Avenue in Borough Park, seemed like the most beautiful sight Kevin had ever seen. Even from the outside he felt that nothing bad could happen to him in a place that was bursting with so much life—so much normal, busy, noisy life.

Cars were double-parked everywhere but near the fire hydrant in front of the entrance; Kevin pulled in at a wide angle to it and sprinted through the front door.

Kevin was somewhat calmed by the boisterous activity and raucous laughter coming from every corner of The Famous. Beards and yarmulkes, business suits and track suits, designer shirts and tank tops: The Famous was part maze and part mosaic. It took a moment before Kevin recognized the figure seated behind a cup of coffee at the front table. Heaving a sigh of relief, Calhoun extended his hand to George, the Intel Detective who headed the mayor's security detachment.

"Jesus, George," Kevin sputtered, "I don't know whether the fact that you're here makes me feel completely safe or completely scares the shit out of me."

George smiled but his tone indicated it was no laughing matter when he said, "Abe called me. I think we've got to assume this is as serious as it looks. So I called Miss Cogan. Gave her the flashing red. Don't worry, we're on her door twenty-four hours. Abe's in the back," George said. "Go ahead, we've got things covered. This is the only way in. The rear's gated."

Kevin smiled wanly as his eye settled on Abe playing pinochle at a table in the back. Abe handed his cards to the waiter, who was kibitzing over his shoulder. "Here, Morty, you've been preparing for this moment all of your life," he teased.

Abe and Kevin went into a huddle in a

corner of the kitchen and Abe asked the cook to please leave them alone for a few minutes. When Kevin began to shake, Abe reached over and put a steadying hand on his arm.

"Schwartz is dead," Kevin blurted out.

"Keep your voice down," Abe admonished.

"For God's sake," Kevin continued in a desperate whisper, "Pathetic little Schwartz. Dead. And the mob is after Marybeth and me. What are we going to do?"

"Get hold of yourself, Kevin," Abe said firmly. "We can't do anything if you don't get a grip on yourself."

But Calhoun could no longer adhere to decorum. "You knew it the day we saw him, didn't you, Abe," he said accusingly. "You were right. You said it wasn't kosher. Turns out there was another report . . . *another* probation report. Why didn't you sound the alarm sooner?"

"I wasn't sure," Abe said evenly. "It was only a feeling I had."

"Well, now it's a fact, isn't it?" Calhoun hissed. "Did you have a feeling that five people were going to end up dead? Maybe five people and counting. And Walter Stern with his white hair, his perfect teeth, his good suits, and his degree from Yale Law is a crook. Where are we going, Abe?"

"I don't have the answer," Abe said humbly. "But we've got to keep going."

"That's the trouble, don't you see?" Kevin said plaintively. This time when Abe reached out to comfort him, Kevin held tightly to his arm. "Give me something, Abe. Give me some help here."

But Abe just sat silently holding Kevin's arm until the deputy mayor had finally come down to a high ordinary level of adrenalin. Without the need for words, calm and strength started to pass back and forth between them. Finally, Kevin recovered himself.

"Thanks, Abe," he said simply as he withdrew his arm and took a sip of coffee. With a challenging smile, Kevin said, "Here's one for you: 'The only thing new in the world is the history you don't know.' "

Abe nodded appreciatively. "I don't know," he said gently. "New Testament?"

"Nah . . . Harry Truman," Kevin answered.

Both men shook their heads and laughed affectionately.

CHAPTER TWENTY

Calhoun found the mayor sitting alon
sively in his small den at Gracie M.
Intel had briefed him on the events leadi.
to Kevin's visit, and for the first time his young
deputy could see the lines of wear and tear
eating into the mayor's brow.

"The bodies are piling up at the fire door.
I'm ready to move, paint the town with sub-
poenas, bring down Judge Stern," the deputy
mayor indicated with a submerged frenzied
enthusiasm at having finally trapped his man.
"What did you think?" he added, almost as an
afterthought to the obvious.

"Walter Stern is a good man," was the may-
or's melancholy reply. What Kevin could not

see were the painful images of good and bad times spent together floating through the mayor's mind. Political death could not eradicate memory. Destroying a friend was not high on John Pappas' agenda, especially one who possessed so many good qualities as Walter Stern.

"Good? Five people are dead," Calhoun pressed relentlessly on.

"I know that. What's your point?" the mayor responded with a fatigue which Kevin could not comprehend from this man who was resilient in even the most heinous circumstances.

"We throw the book at the guy, and you hurry out of the way. Embrace Detective Santos, a medal for the deceased and the max death settlement for the widow," he said with the excitement of a hunter going for the kill. Checking his watch, Kevin proclaimed a sense of urgency. "And we'll see that Leslie makes the morning editions with it."

"You've got it all figured out," Mayor Pappas said in a subdued voice.

"Isn't that my job?" Calhoun responded with a degree of detached pretension.

A tinge of revulsion at his young deputy's excessively honed ambition overcame the old war horse.

"That's cold, Kevin. That's cold." But after

a deep breath, he recovered his mentor's attitude and added, "Isn't it more complicated than that?"

Calhoun's blatant enthusiasm seemed to dampen in the face of Mayor Pappas' troubled reaction.

"Forgive me, I know you're old friends," he said apologetically, while he remained steadfast in his point of view.

"Be careful how you judge people, most of all friends. You think you can sum up a man's life in a moment?" the mayor said in a broken voice. And running a memory tape before his tired eyes, John Pappas continued with the sadness of seeing a dear friend going down under a sentence of capital punishment for a mistake inconsistent with his life force and good works: "There are no cold answers, are there? No simple yes or no. A man's life is not the bricks, it's the mortar, Kevin, it's what lays between." He paused in lonely thought and added: "I've known Walter Stern a long time, he's a good man, a man you could count on. Not some ordinary hack on the bench, but a real judicial mind." The mayor was not trying to persuade his deputy to refrain from acting, as much as to explain the private and public tragedy which was occurring.

"But this is tough stuff, body-bag stuff. Tell me if there's some other way," the deputy mayor put forward with little doubt as to the answer.

Mayor Pappas swallowed his emotion and his eyes were heavy when he bowed to inevitable political reason.

"There isn't. And it was cast a long time ago. Just go easy. Give him a blindfold and have mercy. Walter Stern was tough but he was fair. We'll give him back the same."

Calhoun broke away quickly from the conversation with a victor's satisfaction. Mayor Pappas grabbed Kevin by the arm, adding with genuine concern: "And you be careful. Keep George and Bobby with you at all times."

"I hear you," Calhoun responded running out the door.

Deputy Mayor Calhoun entered the judicial chamber in a lather, prepared to sweat the truth out of a resistant Judge Stern. Instead he found a once-proud man deformed by guilt, feeling that he personally murdered Robby Bone. In his precarious state of mind, Stern believed that his only chance of spiritual redemption was through confession and atonement.

"If only I had stopped when I saw Tino's dead eyes in my courtroom, Robby Bone would still be alive," Judge Stern offered in greeting Calhoun. "My wife asked, 'How could you know?' " he said ruefully. "But I should have expected the unexpected," Stern mumbled twice, staring into the dark futility of remorse.

"I knew when that bullet hit the boy, it would keep traveling," Stern observed, nodding his head over and over.

"And find its way?" Calhoun prodded for details.

"To me. If only it had found me first. If only I could have stepped in front of him." After a long silence, the words dropped like death from his lips: "Regrets are pathetic, aren't they."

"How did it happen?" Calhoun pushed him.

Stern shuddered, his lips trembled, and mist in his eyes removed the last vestige of judicial resolve.

"All I wanted was to do some good. I was tired of being the white-shoe litigator. Defending the eighties go-go boys, polluters, and tax cheats. I wanted to do public service. I needed to help real people. And all it took was fifty thousand dollars to change my life. On Court Street, there had always been a bidding process to become a judge. If I paid a cash campaign contribution the judgeship was mine even though I would run unopposed. I felt honored; there were lots of others less able out there with the same fifty thousand dollars, but the money Anselmo took was mine, because my friend the mayor had insisted I was so qualified. Absurd, isn't it?" Stern said with absolute self-hatred.

"That's what happens when politics perverts process," Calhoun offered with some sympathy for the condemned man.

Stern continually rubbed his throbbing temples, trying to eradicate the stigma of disgrace from his brain, and said, "The law was pure, I thought. I'll go back to the law from high on the bench. But to get there, I paid with my blood, and a brown paper bag. That was the moment. How should I fold the bag? Roll the top down like my mother did for my bologna sandwich on a basketball trip? Ah, if only I remembered what my mother had told me. Or should I fold it neatly? Crumble it perhaps?" Stern asked, torturing himself. "Finally, I just unceremoniously stuffed the cash in a bag on Anselmo's desk. He smiled and called me 'Judge.' I felt I was in a dream, but I left him the money. That was why I went along with the second probation report. First I told Schwartz no. I had questions as to why there was no accompanying original report, why only supervisors signed the one in front of me. Then he told me Anselmo knew Tino personally, that he was told by Anselmo that the defendant was a good kid who deserved a

chance, and that certain people might otherwise cause a judicial scandal by provoking a
probe of my appointment. Your mind can play
tricks by getting you to accept what you know
to be totally wrong, if it avoids the horrors of
public humiliation. So I went along resolving
never again. However, there was no second
proving." The Judge drifted off into insur-
mountable regrets. "That's what did me in,"
he continued. "Anselmo's bag was the River
Styx. When I filled it I was on my way to the
other side. No turning back." Stern slumped
in his chair listlessly, a portrait of abject
misery.

"The mayor has always had the highest re-
gard for you, Judge," Calhoun acknowledged
to this destroyed man.

"And I for him," Stern replied breaking
down into open sobs.

"Your resignation in about six months
would be appropriate," Kevin suggested
quietly.

Judge Stern raised his head from his palms.

"Six months did you say?" Stern asked with
a wan smile, which connoted only woe.

"Yes."

"How about six hours?" Stern said with
commitment, his life force ebbing before the
young deputy mayor.

For the first time Kevin Calhoun had an

adult price to pay. He understood what the mayor had implied about the full private and public tragedy that his determination had wrought, seeing the ruined remnants of a noble person who only wanted to do and could have done much good.

The mayor's office in City Hall was bustling with activity preparing for a press conference to answer questions about Judge Stern's resignation and the mushrooming probation department scandal. Inside the mayor's office, the atmosphere was disconcertingly quiet. Pappas stood behind his desk reading from a draft statement, while Calhoun sat in a chair alongside the desk, alternating between watching the mayor's rehearsal and three TV screens inside a specially built console, which were tuned to the major news programs. The sounds were on mute, but the same uncomfortable images were flashing across each screen: pictures of probation department officials being hauled in for questioning by the district attorney.

"Okay," the mayor finally said, placing the paper on the desk. I think this will work," he pronounced, reading aloud his opening remarks: "Sadly, for unexplainable personal reasons, sometimes a gentleman of impeccable credentials and character fails to live up to the high standard required by his office and the public trust."

The press secretary stuck her head in the door. "The animals are getting hungry," she said.

"Okay, okay," the mayor said. "Give them a 'one minute.'"

Placing the statement into a folder, Pappas turned to Kevin. "I don't need you for the press conference. Get back to work on the convention. Try to keep Senator Marquand on the reservation. Tell him this is just a blip that we're riding through. Tell him all systems are still go for June. Okay?"

"Sure," Kevin replied without much heart.

Standing at the doors to the Blue Room, the mayoral party could hear Leslie shouting, "Thirty seconds," to warn the reporters and cameras of their impending entrance.

The mayor was acting as if someone had died. Seeing Judge Stern go down was like tearing a live piece of flesh from his body, because the mayor knew that despite his political power he was unable to throw his friend a life preserver. And that at his age he couldn't replace a true friend like Walter Stern.

"You sure you're all right?" Kevin said, unable to hide his real concern for the mayor.

"Of course I'm all right," John Pappas responded forcefully. "Damage control, Kevin, damage control," he repeated with professional discipline, but still unable to mask his personal distress.

Sensing that the mayor could use some further reassurance, Kevin smiled and said, "You look good."

"Of course I look good," the mayor boomed with contrived jocularity, "I'm about to give the performance of a lifetime."

Seated in his small office, Calhoun turned on his TV set to the internal feed. He turned the sound down low while he placed a call to Senator Marquand's private number. The Senator himself answered after two rings and, as soon as Kevin identified himself, Marquand got straight to the point.

"What the hell is going on up there? Are you going to be able to put a lid on this business?"

Even while speaking, Calhoun was able to listen to what the mayor was telling his press conference. And he could tell that it sounded good . . . very good.

"Lyndon Johnson said, 'Everybody will give you ideas on how to get out of trouble cheaply and fast and they all come down to this: deny your responsibility,'" the mayor was saying. "John F. Kennedy said, 'An error doesn't have to become a mistake until you refuse to correct it,'" he continued. "Well, we're not going to deny our responsibility to refuse to correct our errors. And by 'we,' I mean 'me.' My administration has had a fever of a hundred and five. Sometimes a fever is a blessing. In medicine, they call it a 'proving.' Well, we're proved out now and we're going to get well."

CHAPTER TWENTY-ONE

Anselmo's neighbors tried to conceal their worry when they saw the Boss making a rare noontime visit to his home. The normally gregarious, affable leader seemed alone and deserted as he slowly got out of his plain Buick sedan. He tipped his hat to a familiar passerby who looked at the ground in helpless discomfort, and then ritualistically waved to local mothers and children who still felt safe playing with snowballs and building snowmen in the streets of this neat middle-class block in Bayridge. As Anselmo entered the house and hung up his overcoat, he could hear the radio from the kitchen:

"There were explosive developments on the

'Carver Houses Incident' this morning," a newscaster said racing through the lead WINS story. "The revelation of an earlier missing probation report which recommended ten to twenty years rather than probation for gangland murderer Tino Zapatti, is expected to result in the handing up of indictments by the Grand Jury of Supreme Court Judge Walter Stern and powerful Brooklyn Democratic Boss Frank Anselmo. Anselmo's connections to Mafia chieftain Paul Zapatti are certain to be examined, and informed sources say the career of the personable political boss is finished and a long prison term is in the offing."

Anselmo snapped the radio off and looked blankly over the pots working on the kitchen stove, when he heard his wife Nettie's voice call from the cellar, "Honey, is that you?"

"I'm home," he replied in a weaker voice than usual, feeling an increased sense of foreboding from the broadcast.

"I'll be right up! I'm having trouble with the dryer!" she shouted, and he could instantly hear the scuffle of footsteps as she hastily mounted the cellar stairs.

Anselmo crossed into a porch, closed up in the winter to make a den, but with a side door that opened to the street. He took his jacket off and sat down lost in thought, a shattered spirit searching the middle distance of these familiar surroundings for a clue to his destiny. He knew this was the big fall from which he could not rise again; Frank Anselmo, Boss of Kings County, Chairman of the New York State Democratic party, was finished.

"You okay?" Nettie asked, alert to their calamity.

"Fine, sweetheart, I'm fine," Frank responded in a faltering voice.

"It's been on the radio all morning," she said softly, seeking some comforting explanation from the man who always gave her strength.

"I know, I heard," was all he could say.

Sensing the futility of more questions, Nettie returned to the simple devotion and kindness that characterized their three decade relationship. "I fixed you some osso bucco," she said.

"Yeah?" Frank responded with the subdued enthusiasm of a man eating his last meal on death row.

"I had a feeling you might come home for lunch," Nettie continued, trying to penetrate his desolation.

"Smells good," was the only answer he could muster from his deepening despair.

"Be right back. I'll just get the clothes, the machine's thunking again."

Anselmo dropped his head against the back

of the couch in exhaustion. As he leaned back, for a terrible moment a shadow fell across his face; he jumped to his feet looking out to see Paul Zapatti himself standing like a specter at the side door to the porch. Anselmo opened the door and greeted the don with a wide embrace.

"Paulie!" was all Frank could manage to utter before the sweat manufactured by terror covered his body.

"How are you, Frank?" Zapatti said with a hypocritical smile that was cut into his waxworks face.

"I'm good, considering," Frank replied with a forced casualness.

"Of course, of course." Zapatti gave Anselmo a jovial pat on the back.

"Coffee? Nettie's just down with the laundry. You'll stay for lunch? Osso bucco," Frank offered, trying to recapture the old relationship with Paulie.

"Osso bucco," Paulie repeated with a gourmet's admiration.

"Nettie fixes it Piemontese—the peppers and everything," Frank followed on until Zapatti cut him off.

"I had my lunch," Zapatti said coolly.

"I'll get coffee"

"No thanks," Zapatti said, in a tone of "let's get down to business" as he sat down in an armchair. Paulie viewed "friends" with detachment; he used them when he needed to and then moved on to others without looking back.

"So what do you think, Frank?" Paulie asked, as if he had his own opinions to offer.

"Same old story. This time it's this guy Calhoun. I never liked him from day one," Frank indicated with a dismissive wave that was an encompassing reference to earlier scrapes survived.

"A purist," Paulie replied, pursing his lips to infer how dangerous these types were.

"Of the worst kind. He's out of here tomorrow," Anselmo threw out with evident bravado.

"I don't think so," Zapatti answered flatly.

"What are you talking about? He's a reed. You push him, he bends," Frank said in a high pitch, sensing a dire turn in their conversation.

"Not this one. This one's a terrier. I had a dog like him once. I went to have him put down—he jumped out of my arms at the vet's and took off for the park. Sometimes I still think I see him out there, watching me . . . gnawing on an old bone," Zapatti elaborated in the hard and indifferent tone of a dictator who saw unlimited risk in someone he couldn't subjugate.

Nettie appeared with the laundry and practically dropped the basket in fright at seeing Paulie in her home. "Oh excuse me," she pleaded, as if a bigger, unspoken matter was at stake.

Zapatti came politely to his feet, "Can I help you with the basket, Nettie?"

"No, no, I didn't know Frank was expecting you," Nettie murmured, chilled to the bone. *"Due expressi?"* she added in rote fashion.

"Maybe later," Zapatti replied with his waxen smile, almost enjoying his friend's trial.

"Ninety-nine out of a hundred times we can beat something like this," Frank blurted out in growing desperation.

"I don't like the odds," Zapatti replied with the implacable haughtiness of a king refusing to even think on the subject.

Anselmo was stunned. He picked up the undisguised implication. Frank knew that Zapatti was indifferent to life and did not accept the inevitable errors in the complex world they operated in, if they even remotely threatened the Family.

"We go back a long way, Paulie," Frank begged, groveling for his life.

"I know. I tried to close the door, Frank. But I couldn't get it shut," Zapatti said in an impersonal manner, seeming to make this an abstract accounting issue, rather than a friend's life.

"What do you want me to do?" Frank asked hesitatingly, with horror convulsing his whole being.

"Take the pressure off yourself. You're no Barry Markoff," Paulie suggested, referring to an old mob-connected political leader who did hard time in a maximum-security prison without ever talking to the FBI.

"What about Barry Markoff?" Anselmo asked, clinging to a distant hope of some way out.

"He did twelve years standing on his head," Paulie replied in the self-congratulatory tone of one who made the right call.

"You don't think I can, Paulie?" Anselmo added, destitute of any answers, but banking on years of service and friendship.

"Here's the thing they'll tell you, you have the key to the cell. But you won't be able to open it without singing. You're a singer, Frank," Zapatti said, with a firm belief that this man could not overcome his basic nature with self-imposed discipline.

"Give me a chance and I'll show you how quiet I can be," Frank prayed, with cold sweat pouring down his body.

"It's out of my hands, Frank. Do the right thing. Make it easy for yourself," Zapatti said in annoyance, impatient that Frank had the audacity to delay compliance with his imperial execution decree.

"Frank, honey, lunch!" Nettie shouted from the kitchen.

"And your family," Zapatti inserted icily, fearing that Anselmo's hopelessness might turn to defiance, if the stakes were not unthinkable.

Zapatti stood up with this pronounced death sentence, as did Anselmo. Paulie kissed his old friend on both cheeks and slithered silently out the door, turning his head once in a nod to make sure that Anselmo knew he had issued a final decree for him, and if necessary, Nettie.

Anselmo's sky was inky gray when Zapatti walked out the porch door. He gasped for breath, his mind wildly racing to find a port. Then self-loathing rage replaced his fear. Deep down he knew that his last deal was a bad deal; there would be no more decisions, persuasions, threats or deals for Frank Anselmo.

Anselmo's self-directed fury grew when his mind's eye beheld his friend Paulie stripped to the fiend he was. Why had he hooked up with Paulie in the first place? Zapatti had befriended him after he was a mighty power broker and added only marginally to his broad political power base. In return he acquired life-and-death power over Anselmo.

Gradually Anselmo's horror turned to grief. Destitute of hope, standing helplessly naked as a newborn child, without any accoutrements of political power, a mysterious calm came over the Boss. He had always prided himself on being able to accept things as they were. It was over. Paulie was a law unto himself and his execution decree was immutable. Anselmo felt that the only pure integrity in his life was the relationship he shared with Nettie; it was appropriate that his last service be for her, because the only thing he had left to give was his life.

Anselmo determinedly began his honorable pilgrimage without a glance backward at the house. His Buick rolled along the Brooklyn-Queens Expressway; the phone rang, he threw a quick look in its direction and left it alone until it stopped. He drove on, until the phone rang again and he picked it up.

"What happened to you?" Nettie implored with serious urgency.

"I called to you. You were down in the basement. I'm going to get a washer at Orchard Supply, it'll stop the thunk. I'll eat when I get home," Anselmo spoke with disingenuous routine.

"Oh? Okay, be careful," she responded, with feminine foreboding, laced in prayer.

"Of course," Anselmo said sympathetically, mustering the old spirited confidence Nettie was used to.

Anselmo hung up and put a tape into the deck, a duet, a baritone and a soprano singing the finale to *Carousel*.

> "When you walk through a storm
> Keep your chin up high
> And don't be afraid of the dark."

He drove off the BQE onto a scenic frontage road overlooking Long Island Sound that he had passed ten thousand times. He parked. The road noise from passing cars conflicted with the song. He raised the window to block out the conflicting sound and started singing along with the tune:

> "At the end of the storm
> Is a golden sky
> And the sweet silver song of a lark."

Anselmo then reached over to the passenger seat, opened a package he had taken with him, wrapped in one of today's tabloids— "ANSELMO SUMMONED—Clubhouse Boss to Appear in Judicial Scandal"—and a .38 rolled out.

Anselmo set the muzzle of the gun against the side of his head. Tears streamed down the cheeks of this man who hadn't wept since childhood as he echoed aloud his final thought, "I'll miss you, Nettie." Anselmo fired. The report was small, like that of a rimshot punctuation to the orchestration of the song, but it was sufficient to splatter his brains and blood over the windshield and side windows.

City Hall was awash in crisis. The mayor's inner circle tried to find some way to cut the Administration's losses from this explosive political scandal. Calhoun was trying to buy time from the *New York Post*.

"I hear you, I know the water keeps rising, Sadler, in fact it's 'up to the floorboards,' as you say. But I promise you, we're bailing out faster than we're taking in."

Abe entered the office and without a word tossed an envelope on Calhoun's desk.

"Sadler, something just came up, let me get back to you when we can talk at length with some answers," Calhoun said hurriedly.

"The PC thought you might want to have a look at the original probation report. It was found in Anselmo's car," Abe explained briefly.

Calhoun removed the original probation report signed by Wakley and fixed his eyes on the signature of Judge Stern's law clerk, Peter Ragan.

Calhoun entered Judge Stern's chambers as Ragan was packing up the office papers.

"Good afternoon, Mr. Calhoun. I'm sorry, but the judge has left for the day," Ragan said politely but dismissively.

"Of course you're sorry," Calhoun replied challengingly, as he slammed the probation report on Ragan's desk.

"This your signature?" he repeated twice, bouncing his forefinger on the stamp.

Ragan regarded Calhoun coolly, almost with disdain.

"We are required to record the receipt of all documents," he replied methodically.

"What about phone calls? You keep a log of phone calls?" Calhoun pressured him.

"Yes," Ragan answered simply.

"Take a minute, please, and look up for me the dates of Frank Anselmo's calls to this office," the deputy mayor insisted, feeling on top of the scent.

"Let it go, Mr. Deputy Mayor. The case is closed. It's only your senseless curiosity dangerously at work now."

"Calls," Calhoun demanded unrelentingly.

"Okay." Regan sighed resignedly. "You're in the wrong pew, Mr. Calhoun. Frank Anselmo never called this office," Ragan offered with quiet relish.

After a terrible silence, eyes stuck on the floorboards, Calhoun asked the question: "What about the mayor?"

Ragan's and Calhoun's eyes then fixed on each other's in silence.

The mayor in his dressing room saw Calhoun observing him in the mirror, as he tied a dark tie to match his charcoal suit.

"Where you been? I was looking for you a half hour ago," the Mayor asked in a tired voice.

"Trying to get through to Senator Marquand," Calhoun answered, indicating failure in his mission.

"Marquand got through to me. They're moving the convention to Miami," the mayor said evenly, almost like it didn't matter much anymore.

"Miami!" Calhoun was astonished.

"They like Miami. Lots of glamour. Madonna and Whoopi Goldberg just bought houses on South Beach, maybe we could nomi-

nate them," Mayor Pappas injected face-
tiously.

"But the deal was all cut," Calhoun said,
reflecting on the dinner with Senator Marquand.

"Nothing is cut, it's politics," the mayor
preached, as if it was a redundant lesson
given before.

"Where are you going?" Kevin asked, noting
the staid attire.

"To pay my respects to Nettie Anselmo,"
he whispered with eyelids dropping in sad
remembrance of Frank.

"Do you think that's wise?" the deputy may-
or's tone advised clearly against it.

The mayor stopped dressing.

"Frank was a friend of mine. What's 'wise'
got to do with it?" the mayor said, disgusted
that anyone would think that a person could
obliterate the obligations of friendship and
memory.

"But the perception will be—" Kevin continued, going down the road of practical politics until he was abruptly interrupted.

"Fuck perception! We're talking *menschkeit*;
What happens between men. The 'there' that's
there. The thousand telephone calls. The bou-
quets and the brickbats. The space between a
handshake. What goes with you to your
grave," Mayor Pappas hit back with the

melancholy of one who was fed up with the frigid modernism of Kevin Calhoun types.

"Is there space between a handshake for right and wrong?" the Deputy asked hesitatingly.

"Why are you pressing me tonight?"

"I'm looking for an answer," replied Calhoun, becoming more venturesome once on the trail.

The mayor paused reflectively, and then offered low key instruction for the young man.

"Okay, Kevin, think of it as colors. There's black, there's white, but in between it's mostly gray. Gray is a tough color, not so simple as black or white. And for the media, not as interesting. But it is who we are."

"What are you going to do now?" Kevin inquired, chumming the waters to attract conversation.

"You mean we, don't you?"

" 'We?' *We* shot a bear," Calhoun came back.

The mayor's head jerked toward Calhoun with an agitated stare.

"An old Bayou expression I learned in Congress."

"Yeah, and the river's rising, and the water's coming over the levee, but we're piling up the sandbags. We're going to fight the sons of bitches, we're going to come out swinging, we're going to tell them we're only human, everybody makes mistakes. Frank Anselmo is dead, he was a friend but the last of the old clubhouse bosses is gone. We'll clean the Augean stables, we'll show up in Miami, we'll have them on their knees begging me to make the keynote speech," he said in fiery terms that invoked the familiar spirit of his past.

"And then?" Calhoun asked, with noticeable distance.

"A short sojourn in Albany, to be followed by a long one in the White House," the mayor offered, as if rehashing lines from a show that closed last night.

Calhoun blinked.

"I want to tell you that if I didn't know better, I would be bursting with admiration. I thought I'd come here to find you on your knees—instead I see you ready to turn 'adversity' into 'triumph,'" Calhoun responded, as if he had rehearsed the lines and now was devoted to following his script.

"Reflex. An old habit of mine. But I like the way you said that. To know you still believe in me."

"Did I say that?" he wondered aloud in a voice filled with skepticism.

The mayor took a guarded turn toward his deputy.

"I thought you had. Don't fathers listen to their sons?" he said, no longer preoccupied with himself and bringing fresh focus to the conversation. And after a quizzical pause, Pappas asked, "Where is your father these days?"

"In some arid corner of Morocco, I think. Probably die alone in one of those unmapped mummy warehouses some day."

"Don't be too hard on him. We can't dictate our finishes," the mayor uttered almost sorrowfully.

Calhoun measured him in silence. "I don't like the sound of that," he observed.

"Why should you? Because under all that need to believe, all that concrete you've poured into my pedestal, way down in the deepest reaches of your soul, something is struggling to cry out," the mayor suggested.

"What?" Calhoun's voice asked, turning from aggression to outright fear.

"You know I made that phone call to Walter Stern," the mayor said with helpless regret. And after a reflective silence, he continued. "Anselmo called me. Said Stern was my responsibility. Needed a once-in-a-lifetime service to help a decent kid and the good judge was rigidly defying him. I had a hundred vital matters on my plate, didn't think twice about the name Zapatti when I scribbled it down and called Walter." The mayor lowered his head and stood in silence; tightened his lips and shook his head. "And that's all there was to it. A little favor. I've been running caution lights all my life."

"But this time you ran a red. Someone cut across the intersection. A cop and a six-year-old child," the deputy mayor rebutted sternly.

"That's with me forever," the mayor said genuinely begging for personal understanding from his protégé.

"Not good enough."

"Not good enough? Don't you think I know it's not good enough!" John Pappas said mellowly, exhibiting profound disappointment in his deputy's blind focus on his shortcomings.

"I hope so, John," he muttered in disillusion.

A moment passed in gray silence.

"It scares me when you call me John."

"Yeah? Why?" the deputy asked almost in rebellion.

"Because when we were taking that trip to the White House a few minutes ago, I felt you come on board. The old *menschkeit*," the mayor suggested with modest conviction. He knew that you could invite someone and still have him simply say no.

"Horseshit. *Menschkeit* is horseshit. It's business as usual. It's a wink and a poke with the elbow and make him your friend and then we can do business. It's a hundred and twenty years of graft and sweetheart contracts and featherbeds and inside information and golden parachutes and everywhere that people in power gather to carve up the territory. It's the gold-headed cane of Tammany that Boss Tweed used to carry and the toy bank I found in the archives the other day. A tin replica of Boss Tweed, it's a mechanical marvel, you place a coin in his right hand, he nods his head, and drops it in his pocket. And guess what? It still works. That's your *menschkeit*. You know where you can put it. Or maybe spread it over the fields. And if we all cross our fingers and get a little rain, maybe a flower will grow," Calhoun presented in a steely tone, intending to rip the mask from his mentor's face.

A terrible moment passed and the mayor leaned towards Calhoun.

"But it has, hasn't it?" he said softly.

Calhoun remained silent and Pappas went on,

"Out of all of this crap, you'll emerge. Don't you see you're the only voter I've ever cared about? A constituency of one."

"I'm getting the con feeling, John, the old copping of a plea," Calhoun interjected cynically.

"No plea. Nothing. Just a pol who kept rolling along—until he ran into a stone wall. You were that wall. At first I chalked it up to a

Catholic schoolboy's sense of justice, but then I realized nothing was going to stop you. And I knew I was looking at myself when I was young. Ambitious, a go-getter, but fair. Doing good, trading up of course, but always for the right cause. But then after a thousand trades, a deal here, a deal there, the shine in that mirror starts to tarnish. You keep trying to conjure it back because you know the things you are doing are good. You're not trying to put any money in your pocket, you just need to maintain your position. Your *power*. What good are you to the people without it?" He paused weighed down by sadness and fatigue.

"But down deep you know there's a line you can't cross," Pappas hesitated, reflecting on how key moments in life, indeed in civilization, go off on chance.

"Somehow, one day, after a thousand trades, and one deal too many, the line gets rubbed out."

"At least there was one once," Kevin retorted unforgivingly.

The mayor drew a curtain and stood looking at the trees in Gracie Park that branched out over the high-rises looming above them. "Of course there was," he continued. "I had the fire in the belly, just like you. The odd thing is it's never left me. Look at me! What do you see? Some greasy Latino from Brooklyn or am

I Pericles? Am I a father of a city-state or just another bum like Jimmy Walker or Bill O'Dwyer? I'm not. I swear to you I'm not. I saw this city as the center of the universe and I thanked God every day for letting me lead it. I had the dream and I had the weight. As Koch said before me, 'If a sparrow dies in Central Park, I am responsible.' Well said. I feel that way. And I was ready to carry that torch right down to Washington. Oh, the things I could have done," the mayor said with the sadness of one who was committed to building a city for men and women, but would now abandon the task incomplete by even his own possibilities.

"Yes, the things you could have done," Kevin now said in a voice that recognized the public and private tragedy. A lifetime, minus a moment, created total defeat.

"It's time for an exit. I'm going to announce I will not run for re-election, and that I'm resigning to allow the Democratic Party to groom my successor for re-election." And he continued looking at Kevin, "I thought I'd see a boy's tears, instead I feel a man's spine."

"The tears are there. On the inside. You just can't see them right now," Calhoun murmured, indicating that again he recognized that he was participating in a tragedy for his mentor and the City.

The mayor reached out for Calhoun. At first Calhoun froze, then relaxed, and they embraced each other fiercely. The mayor whispered in his protégé's ear, "You've got the stuff, Kevin. I love to see it in a guy."

Mayor Pappas turned without another word and left Calhoun standing alone. The deputy mayor wondered dejectedly to himself, "If John Pappas and Walter Stern couldn't beat the system, could anyone?"

EPILOGUE

NEW YORK ONE YEAR LATER

Thousands of straphangers returning from work poured continually out of the Seventy-second Street and Broadway subway station to a political greeting from loudspeakers mounted on a minivan covered with election posters: "Voters of the twenty-first district, you can make a difference," it blared, "Vote for Kevin Calhoun for the City Council."

Kevin Calhoun stood in the mouth of the underground trying to buttonhole as many of the emerging passengers as he could touch. Three college volunteers surrounded him, one pumping a poster on a thin wooden stick, another shouting, "Come meet your next councilman," and the third sheepdogging passersby who looked up toward shaking hands with their candidate. Another two teenagers aggressively thrust leaflets into any hand that opened when its torso brushed by, and not too many hands did; some let the leaflets drop to the ground after a glance, while a few actually said thank you and stuffed them in their pockets for future reference. At the farthest point of the subway entrance, a young girl gave away shopping bags imprinted "CALHOUN FOR COUNCILMAN, 21ST DISTRICT." A few especially aggressive women demanded two, with the excuse they needed "one more for a friend."

For each hand shaken, ten pushed by, ignoring Kevin. The former deputy mayor's eyes came alive when a middle-aged lady emerged from the rush hour mob carrying a Calhoun shopping bag she had received in the morning. Practically grinning with enthusiasm at this discrete little sign, he warmly shook her hand and said, "Thanks. I'm counting on you." And he quickly reached out with his hand to the gentleman behind her. "Hi, Kevin Calhoun. I'll be working only for you." And without missing a beat he turned to another and grabbed her hand. "Hi, Kevin Calhoun, I need your vote."

While the former deputy mayor worked the

crowd, Abe and Mayor Pappas' former press secretary, Leslie, continued to input the minivan's sound system with campaign talk.

"So has he got it?" Leslie asked taking a momentary respite.

"He's got it, maybe not this November, but maybe the next, and if not then, then the one after," Abe replied with conviction.

"I don't know if I can wait that long," Leslie said mocking her own impatience.

"As the Talmud says, 'God waits long but pays with interest,'" Abe suggested, combining religion with practical politics.

"You mean you really have a stomach for this all over again?" she asked, partially talking to herself.

"Granted I counted only twelve heads in a union hall last night, it made me nauseous," Abe said with a little boy, 'so-what-can-I-do-to-help-myself' smile.

"From little acorns, mammoths grow," Leslie laughed recollecting a grade-school saying.

"The man doesn't get discouraged, he's got a nice smile and no longer does he linger in abstract theory," Abe said taking an accounting with his eyes of Calhoun's campaign style.

"I see the bug's bit you good. Me too," Leslie said somewhat surprised.

"And a few others. They're signing on. They asked him to speak at the firehouse tonight, tomorrow the Catholic high school, even the right-wingers are taking a shine to him," he said, laughing at the very modest horde he described in this huge city.

"You think we've hooked our wagon to a star, Abe?" Leslie put on her groupie look skyward.

"Star, shmar—in a city where there are no men, he strives to be a man," Abe responded seriously, summing up a lengthy evaluation.

"No small thing," Leslie agreed.

"No, no small thing," Abe echoed looking into the future.

The victim is found facedown in a plate of spaghetti. It's the first in a series of unspeakable crimes so depraved and twisted that even veteran city cops can't look at them. And each murder comes with a name: this one is gluttony.

Somerset doesn't want this case. The city's best homicide cop, he's just one week from retiring—a week he planned to spend training his replacement David Mills, a real pain-in-the-butt go-getter. But after the second murder, Somerset knows there's a madman out there, one promising to avenge all seven deadly sins—and only he and Mills can stop him....

SEVEN

**THE ELECTRIFYING NOVEL
BY ANTHONY BRUNO—
BASED ON THE BLOCKBUSTER MOTION PICTURE
STARRING BRAD PITT AND MORGAN FREEMAN**

Alcatraz. The prison fortress off the coast of San Francisco. No man had gotten out alive before his time was up, until a 20-year-old petty thief named Willie Moore broke out.

Recaptured, then thrown into a pitch-black hellhole for three agonizing years, Willie is driven to near-madness—and finally to a brutal killing. Now, up on first-degree murder charges, he must wrestle with his nightmares and forge an alliance with Henry Davidson, the embattled lawyer who will risk losing his career and the woman he loves in a desperate bid to save Willie from the gas chamber.

Together, Willie and Henry will dare the most impossible act of all: get Willie off on a savage crime that the system drove him to commit—and put Alcatraz itself on trial.

MURDER
IN THE FIRST

DAN GORDON

NOW A MAJOR MOTION PICTURE STARRING CHRISTIAN SLATER, KEVIN BACON, AND GARY OLDMAN

MURDER IN THE FIRST
Dan Gordon
_____ 95532-4 $4.99 U.S./$5.99 CAN.

Publishers Book and Audio Mailing Service
P.O. Box 120159, Staten Island, NY 10312-0004
Please send me the book(s) I have checked above. I am enclosing $ _____ (please add $1.50 for the first book, and $.50 for each additional book to cover postage and handling. Send check or money order only—no CODs) or charge my VISA, MASTERCARD, DISCOVER or AMERICAN EXPRESS card.

Card number _____

Expiration date _____ Signature _____

Name _____

Address _____

City _____ State/Zip_____
Please allow six weeks for delivery. Prices subject to change without notice. Payment in U.S. funds only. New York residents add applicable sales tax.   FIRST 3/95